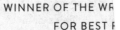

"Season Butler has written an imaginative, atmospheric, and original novel that lingers in the memory long after reading. She is a bright new voice in literature."　　—Bernardine Evaristo, author of *Girl, Woman, Other*

"*Cygnet* is a powerful, poignant, smart debut novel by Season Butler. Her protagonist, known only as Kid, lives on an island otherwise populated entirely by elderly separatists. . . . With the house literally falling out from under her, Kid will have to face her own future, create it for herself. By the end, this feels like a situation we all have in common."　　—*Shelf Awareness*

"*Cygnet* is a beautiful book, a meander through the fluid anxiety of youth, an observation of fixed imperfections of age, and a longing search for compassion on the journey between."
　　—Uzodinma Iweala, author of *Speak No Evil* and *Beasts of No Nation*

"Teenage 'Kid' is abandoned by her parents on an island community of elderly citizens who don't want her around. She scrambles to survive under adverse circumstances. You can't help but root for this resourceful but vulnerable girl who yearns for her parents' return."　　—*Minneapolis Star Tribune*

"Terribly moving. A clear-sighted, poignant rumination on loneliness, love, the melancholy of age and of youth—and, in its quiet way, the end of the world."　　—China Miéville, author of *Perdido Street Station*

"Butler's writing is sensitive and sharp. . . . Climate change beats in the background, as incessant as the ocean waves eating away at Swan Island. There's a metaphor to be found in Kid's obsession with the deteriorating island while the [other inhabitants] remain unfazed. . . . A unique debut from a promising writer."　　—*Kirkus Reviews*

"Butler has created an appealingly rich world with quirky, flawed characters and a dramatic landscape determined by the constant action of wind and water. Butler delivers a potent and finely calibrated novel."   —*Publishers Weekly*

"Not since Holden Caulfield have I been so captivated by a first-person voice as the one Season Butler creates in *Cygnet*. . . . This sad, funny, highly original novel keeps us turning the pages."
        —Blake Morrison, author of *And When Did You Last See Your Father?*

"[A] beautifully off-kilter debut. . . . Through excellent writing, Butler has created a wonderfully bizarre . . . novel filled with quirky characters and a heroine to root for. Readers will want to keep their eyes on Butler."   —*Booklist*

"Season Butler is an extraordinary writer. In this wonderful novel the narrative voice is rhythmic and compelling, telling a coming-of-age story that resonates with our times. Like Colson Whitehead, her work is fearless in its inventiveness."   —Julia Bell, author of *Massive*

UK PRAISE

"An original novel with a memorable narrator."
        —*Elle*, "Eight Books to Devour"

"[A] potent debut. . . . A strange, promising beginning."   —*The Guardian*

"Kid's ardent voice powers *Cygnet*. Her expression of the loneliness, boredom, and rage she feels at her circumstances is reminiscent of Holden Caulfield . . . the characters have real emotional depth. . . . *Cygnet* is both very funny and convincingly tragic, its young narrator memorably charismatic and self-aware."   —*Literary Review*

"The narrator['s] wise reflections on age, race, class, and global warming belie her tender youth."   —*New Internationalist*

"An uncanny meditation on mortality and intergenerational distrust."   —*Metro*

"[A] vivid, poetic debut."   —*Daily Mail*

Cygnet

Cygnet

A Novel

SEASON BUTLER

HARPER  PERENNIAL

NEW YORK • LONDON • TORONTO • SYDNEY • NEW DELHI • AUCKLAND

HARPER PERENNIAL

Originally published in the United Kingdom in 2019 by Dialogue Books, an imprint of Little, Brown UK.

A hardcover edition of this book was published in 2019 by HarperCollins Publishers.

FIRST HARPER PERENNIAL EDITION PUBLISHED 2021.

Library of Congress Cataloging-in-Publication Data has been applied for.

ISBN 978-0-06-309591-5

21 22 23 24 25   LSC   10 9 8 7 6 5 4 3 2 1

For my sisters.

Cygnet

CHAPTER ONE

I open my eyes to the churning of the waves outside. They don't rest, so I don't sleep well either. I really should be used to it by now. At least it's sunny. I try to use the thought to power my move out of bed and into my clothes and off to Mrs. Tyburn's house for work. To be honest, I preferred it last week when it rained every day. Rain in big wet slaps, the kind of rain you only get on islands, out to sea. On dark mornings there's a reason why it's hard to get up, an actual weight in the air to fight, something real to run from, to hide your face from. Today it's clear and the light is coming through my window like the blond arm of a Christmas card angel. But fuck you, I don't want to go.

The clothes I washed yesterday should be dry by now, out on the clothesline strung between two trees in the backyard. I don't have a lot to choose from clothes-wise now that it's summer, so I do laundry kind of a lot. It's too hot for most of the clothes I packed to come here, when I thought this would only be for a week or two. That's what my parents said when they left me on my grandmother's old folks' island—just a week or two, a month at the most, and we'll come get you. My mother kissed me with those purple-brown lips of hers and said, "We'll be right back, hold tight."

Those dickheads are always late.

And the old folks, the Swan Island Swans, are past caring whether I have anywhere to go. Most of them didn't care in the first place, were reluctant to agree to my coming here at all. By now they just want me gone.

As I walk through the house, it's easy to ignore the mess I've left. There's a path from the stairs and into the kitchen and to the back door where that too-bright morning becomes big and real and takes over my field of vision. When I close my eyes, I can make the ocean sound like a city. Swells of traffic and millions of voices that flow together into a murmur. I walk toward it as if to an overpass at the edge of a highway. Normal people don't live like this.

I open my eyes and try to judge how close to the edge I can go. I stop a couple of yards shy of the edge and look over into the waves. From my bed it didn't sound this bad. I almost managed to pretend that I had dreamt it. No such luck. Another few feet of the cliff are gone. The end of the yard is a booby trap, something out of a cartoon. There's no ground under the grass, nothing underneath to support your weight, just a drop into the constant traffic of the waves against the rocks. Fresh rock and soil and dangling roots like the nerves of an extracted tooth are exposed along the C-shaped underside of the cliff face. The clothesline and the few things I had left to wear in this weather are long gone. One of the trees, a dogwood, clings to the cliff side at a desperate angle, four-petaled blossoms shivering in the wind. It looks like it's still falling. I can't see the other one at all. My dogwood tree at the bottom of the sea.

One, two, three, four. A few more steps and I could end this. Five, six, seven, the end.

Shit. Oh, shit, Mom, where are you?

Staring out toward the ocean makes my heart beat hard, like it's being punched by someone I can't see, someone who really hates me. But it's also hard to pull myself back from the edge. I'm trying to figure this out, trying to get my head around how to retrieve the trees and the land and my clothes. How to make this process change its mind. It's upsetting, and stupid. Confusing in a different way from anything else. Confusing down into my bones.

I pad back through the house and take the stairs two at a time. In my room (the guest room actually) there's nothing on the walls except the watercolors Lolly used to do at an evening class in the chapel. When I told her I liked them, she just rolled her eyes. She was right, of course, they're no great shakes, and it was good to have someone who didn't need to be lied to all the time. I always thought I could be like her if only I studied her carefully enough, watched her closely and memorized her, but she always seemed too far away to see clearly.

Wool pants, a thermal hoodie, some sweaters spreading across the floor. Winter stuff. Nothing I can wear today. But they'll be back soon. Probably tomorrow, even. They'll have to.

Pushing eight-thirty. The last of my clean work clothes are gone and there's nothing I can do about it. I have to borrow something of Lolly's. I find myself tiptoeing as I cross the landing that separates my room and hers. She hated it when I went into her room. I didn't see what the big deal was, but she caught me in there once borrowing socks and she turned and left all freaked out like she'd just caught me mixing up a cocktail of perfume and hand sanitizer. I came downstairs with an apology all ready but she'd gone and left one of her weird little notes. Something like, *I'm happy to lend you anything you need but you really must ask. I love you.*

She always said that. And she did, I guess. She just didn't want me.

The carpet in her room is softer than in the rest of the house. Her bed is made tightly, like if Laura Ashley ran the army. Simple dark-wood bedside table with nothing on it but a Tiffany lamp, pretty stained-glass shade anchored in place with an iron base. In its single drawer are her reading glasses, her bible, a little pack of tissues, a pen and a pad with four or five pages ripped out, half a roll of cough drops, her checkbook (don't get excited, it doesn't work; I tried using it in February for the mortgage payment but the bank noticed the forged signature and sent the check back), a bottle of Valium, and three first-class stamps. After she made it clear I wasn't to go into her room, I just had to, every chance I got. There are six Valium left. I take one and place the bottle exactly where it was.

Her closet smells of lavender and cedar. Everything is clean and pressed and hanging with similar garments in similar colors. This is probably better anyway; I always look grubby in my own clothes, even when they're just washed, and Mrs. Tyburn looks at me differently when I look grubby. She never actually says any-thing, which kind of makes it worse.

I grab a red skirt that feels light enough for the weather and a black button-down shirt with sleeves I can roll up, and stop when I see the neat handwriting on the Post-it note on the closet door. *Moths, do not leave open.* I obey and dash back to my room, willing my feet not to press dents into her carpet.

A cymbal clap of wind and waves outside sends the crumbling cliff to the front of my mind's eye, making my nerves too brittle to meet up the buttons with their holes. It's okay. I'll be able to leave soon. They promised they wouldn't leave me here for long. And anyway I'm going to move back to New York, just as soon as I save up enough for the deposit on an apartment. But with the mortgage here and the bills I never have much left over. Eventually, though. Soon. I won't be able to afford a place by myself, but it could be cool to have roommates. Sometimes I rehearse what it would be like. I wouldn't want to make things awkward by acting eager or too withdrawn. I would keep to myself just enough. Let them take the lead until I figure out how much space people my age want. Will we hang out and cook together, or go out to our local bar and sit in the same spot every time? Talk about bands and, I don't know, something quirky like classic cars or paleo baking? Not that I know anything about anything, but I could catch up. They'd see me as the quiet one, a little weird but a good person really. *Once you get to know her.* I could fit in.

Down in the kitchen I pull a paper towel off the roll and cut a wedge of the apple pie I made yesterday. Congealed and tart and sweet, it makes the perfect breakfast eaten out of hand in the dash to Mrs. Tyburn's house. I stuff a bite into my mouth and wrap the dish with the remaining pie, a generous half, in a kitchen towel, then hoist my bag onto my shoulder and pull the kitchen door shut behind me.

As usual, the waves are waiting.

I think most people have some part of their neighborhood where they never go—an uninspiring park, a corner where men sit and make noise when you walk by, the yard where a dog barks and lunges and flings ropes of froth from its gums, the street where the cars go slow and stop without really parking, and the transactions are quick and furtive. For me, that part of the neighborhood is the sea. I leave it alone and it leaves me alone. Except that, lately, it doesn't.

I try not to look over my shoulder and across my shrunken backyard. I'm pretty good at it, after six months of practice. I keep my eyes forward as I head around the house, or look down at the stumpy green and brown spikes of grass and choose my path carefully as I walk up the little hill, because the steps that are there to make it easier to walk up are wrecked and do the opposite of what they're there for. But obviously my mind hates me and when I get to the top of the hill where the path to my house meets the road, my head twists and I glance behind me and everything stops.

I feel ungrateful, but I hate it so much, this view, this breathtaking view. Most people would think I'm lucky to have it. I am, I know, but I hate it. It's like falling through noise. Christ, the ocean makes so much noise. It's like a jet engine. But no one complains because the ocean is beautiful and beauty lets you get away with murder. My chest closes up, I turn my back to it, but the noise persists. It keeps coming, and even though I can't breathe I somehow have to outrun it while it roars at me, drooling with its hunger to swallow me up.

I take the hill in long, tense strides, every step a trade-off between speed and balance, keeping the pie from falling, keeping myself upright, holding it together. I rest at the top of the hill and force my face in the other direction, to the middle of the island. I can just about make out the point of the steeple. Not far from here, but as far from the ocean as it gets. The Valium is kicking in. My shoulders retreat away from my ears, and when I get my wind back, and the sweat on my skin starts to cool, I press on.

Lolly's house is secluded on the south side of the island. I've long since finished my slice of pie and squeezed the napkin into a hard little ball by the time I reach my nearest neighbor's house. It belongs to a Wrinkly called Nick. I square my hips with his front door and hold my offering in front of me in a way I hope is appealing. His house is just like mine but further from the cliff. It will go over someday, but mine will go first. That timeline would be all wrong back in the Bad Place, but here it's perfectly fair.

Two stories, simple shingled roof, white wooden siding, freshly raked gravel path from the door to the entrance. Big windows like curious eyes gaze out at the passerby. I force myself to walk to the door against all my better judgment.

I knock. No answer. I look at my feet and rub some dust off my ankle with my opposite instep. I lift my fist to knock again but think better of it. Instead, I move my face to press my ear against the door. As it makes contact with the paint, sticky in the rising summer heat, the door swings open and I stumble into Nick's big, furry chest, which is blotchy pink and peeling in places where he's sunburned. Somehow I manage not to drop the pie.

I straighten and wait for him to say something but he just stands his ground and lifts his chin to its highest point, expecting me to speak first. My tongue fills my mouth and won't coordinate with my thoughts.

"Yes?" he says finally, brows lifted, mouth pursed.

My mouth just hangs open. I think I'm trying to smile. I'm sure I look ridiculous.

I hold up the pie. "I made this but I can't finish it on my own, so I thought you might like half?"

"Leftovers!" He makes his voice high in sharp mock excitement. "How nice of you to offer, but I don't eat junk food. You understand."

I look away from the glare of his blue eyes as the sticky door slams in my face; I understand perfectly. It was stupid of me to come here. Peace offerings are pointless coming from the side that's already lost. Why can't he see that I just need a little more time? I'm not old enough to be here, sure. Not by a long shot. But I'm not trying to ruin their retirement paradise; I'm waiting for my folks. Trying to be good and quiet and patient. Still, everything I do just seems to make things worse.

I'll bring the rest of the pie to Rose. She'll be happy to have it, maybe even proud of me for how well the crust came out. Might even give me a hug or something, if no one else is in her shop.

Nick's the worst of the really hard-core separatists. Some of the Wrinklies make a show of ignoring me or take exaggerated swerves to avoid me. What's worse than that, worse than the shitty little digs Nick will lob at me every chance he gets, are the ones who *tolerate* me, like they deserve the Nobel fucking Peace Prize for exercising the self-control it takes not to shit on a kid who's probably an orphan for all they know. Nick's the most aggressive for sure. Before he ever even spoke to me directly I overheard him in the chapel talking to Mrs. Tyburn about me:

"She clearly *is* talented, Maude. She's somehow managed to turn two weeks into three months. I mean, *I* thought that's what we agreed. The minutes of the meeting say *two* weeks, *six* at the most. And here we are, *three months* on, and I know I'm not the only one wondering when we get our island back. No disrespect to Violet, but I don't see anything in our charter about compromising our vision to run an orphanage for the offspring of every deadbeat who can't clean up and get on with it. I mean, enough is enough, surely . . ."

And I'm like, right, *that's* my talent, getting dumped on Swan and losing everyone who means anything to me. As if I could be anywhere in the world doing whatever I want, and I picked this place, an idiotic rock in the middle of nowhere, irritating the elderly with the fact that I exist. Living next door to some ugly curmudgeon giving me constant side-eye. Calling hospitals and distant relatives and their friends, scanning cameras and police reports and obituaries. Paying the bank for a house that has a death wish and trying to sweep the crumbs left behind into my future. The big bone at the base of my neck ached against the pew I was sunken down into.

Patches of dandelions poke their jagged leaves and rough little heads out along the edge of the dirt road. The closed buds of the new blossoms look like chapped lips puckering for a kiss no one wants. Dust and sweat are forming streaks of mud on the soles of my grandmother's shoes.

My mother was going to show me how to make dandelion wine, once when I was a kid, but it didn't work out. We lived in Colorado then. One of my dad's friends was starting a business, something to do with telecoms or internet phones or something, and he was going to get us in *on the ground floor*. Turned out to be just another stupid pyramid scheme. We'd packed up and moved two thousand miles for a scam, but that's the thing with my folks. They hear what they want to hear.

Colorado was where I realized that there are places where people don't ignore each other to be polite, or even just give you a quick smile and nod if they've seen you around; they give you an entire sentence, a whole *Have a good day*, or whatever. I've lived in places where that practically constituted an assault. Having someone be that nice to you, out of nowhere, it's almost like being touched. Most of the Swans are at least polite like that. Not Nick; he acts like even waving to me would make his hands dirty.

Anyway, we only lived in Colorado for a sec; I didn't even register for school or anything. But I was there long enough to learn that you don't have to get all bent out of shape whenever a stranger says hi or, like, *howdy*. Money was tight from the move, so my mom and I went out in the afternoons to the overgrown edges of parks and wild spots by the foothills to gather anything edible we could find. Nettles and lamb's-quarters mostly, enough random leaves for a salad, and there was always plenty of mint she'd make into pesto that I never had the heart to tell her that I hated, which she'd mix up with rice or pasta from the charity bin at the local church.

There was this one day in particular—spring was dragging its feet, bright enough to fool you into a T-shirt, making your knees and elbows tight from shivering by the end of the day. We hauled a couple of plastic shopping bags each, strangers nodding or waving or saying hello as we made our way home. We took a different route back and I suspected we were lost, but it didn't matter. At some point we came across a vacant lot full of wildflowers; some of the weeds had grown as tall as my eye line. My mother waded through up to her hips and I followed in the path she made. She pointed out inverted cones of soft, broad leaves tapering into long points at the top covered in little yellow blossoms, dangerous spiky stalks with frayed leaves and short strands of flowers like brittle brown beads, star-shaped blue flowers nestled in dark green foliage near the chain-link fence. "*Verbascum thapsus*, *urtica dioica*, borage for courage." She couldn't remember the Latin name of the last one, but I was impressed anyway.

The dandelions were concentrated around some splintered wooden pallets and scattered through patches of grass and dock leaves. She pulled two more bags out of her pocket: one for the leaves, which she'd cook with the other greens, and one for the blossoms, which we'd use to make wine. It sounded like something out of an old-fashioned fairy tale, something a goblin would drink or that a woodsman would offer the miller's daughter. We only picked the ones with fully opened flowers; she said it was impolite to bother the closed ones. She pinched the base of the stems with her long fingers, deftly, like someone playing a harp. It didn't occur to me then that we must have looked like the strangest kind of bums, not even sifting through trash but gathering nature's rejects on a worthless plot of land through a minor city's smog. I ignored the clumps of half-pulped newspaper and cigarette butts and beer cans, and focused instead on the odd ladybug and the butterflies and the bees; I tried my best to stay in the story, a knee-high apprentice to the wise old master. Once we'd picked all we could within the bounds of fairyland propriety, my mother straightened up and walked us home with an air of confidence she could put on easily back then.

The little house we lived in only had one bedroom so I had to be sure not to get up at night in case my parents were having sex on the couch, but I liked that the kitchen opened onto a small backyard. We sat outside as the sun went down and separated the flowers from the stems, rinsed them, and let the water run off into the grass. She ground the mint down into a paste for the pesto while I boiled the rice. She sautéed the greens while I tossed the salad. And then my dad came in. He slammed the front door, and then the bedroom door. My mother stopped and listened. The bedroom door slammed again.

He charged into the kitchen, almost frantic with confusion. "Where are all the boxes?"

"Boxes?"

I knew what he meant, and I knew I had to answer him, but it was hard to think. "Outside," I coughed finally.

"Where?" He glanced out the window to the backyard.

"No, I mean, you told me to take the trash out last night."

"You threw them away?"

"I thought you told me to."

"So I tell you to do something, and you can't use *any* common sense? Do you think moving boxes are free, that I have nothing but time and money to get new boxes?"

"I didn't think . . ."

"That's right, you didn't. You just don't *think*, do you? Huh?"

He's pressing me for an answer but I don't understand what I did wrong. I try to say yes, try to admit whatever he's accusing me of, but my body feels totally solid and nothing comes. Looking back, I can see that it was probably the casper or tina talking, but I was only twelve or something, and it wouldn't have helped to know that he was just on an aggressive high, because I couldn't walk away from him, not when he was chewing me out and especially not when he was as lit as that.

Just as he growled, "Answer me when I ask you a question," my mother handed me a stack of plates and forks and nudged me out of the line of fire to set the table for dinner. She made a plate for me, shiny fried mixed greens, a green dollop of rice coated in sharp mint pesto, and a frizzy green handful of leaves that passed as a salad in our house, and asked my father if she could speak to him outside.

He paused in the doorway, not quite finished with me. "*Eat your dinner.*" He slammed the kitchen door behind him and the bag with the dandelion blossoms spilled onto the floor. I thought maybe I should go and pick them up but I didn't dare get out of my seat. To the muffled noise of my parents trying to keep their voices down outside, I conjured up unhelpful images of the lot the dandelions came from—the pile of dog shit with loads of flies and a couple of wasps swarming all over it, the stale yeasty smell from a pile of cans, the clump of weeds I stepped in that released a must of cat piss. I concentrated on the hum of their fight and breathed after every bite, determined not to be sick.

Soon their voices were harder to detect. I turned cautiously and saw them through the kitchen window. She was speaking, holding his face and looking into his eyes, then kissing his chin and his cheeks. He lowered his head onto her chest and she held him while he sobbed.

Dad stepped in the puddle of dandelions when they came in, but before he could get angry, my mother put her hand on his shoulder and whispered, "Never mind." She cupped her hand, swept them back into the bag, and threw them away.

They joined me at the table, and we ate in silence. My mother told me to clean up, and she and my father gathered up the things we'd bothered to unpack, put them into trash bags, and loaded the car. We'd been driving for an hour or so before I asked my mother where we were going. She told me to hush.

———

On Swan, the houses get closer to each other the further inland you get, and soon it starts to look almost like a normal town. A small town, obnoxious in that cute New England way. Some of the houses are original from the time the island was first settled. The Wrinklies love to tell me stories about the island's history, only it's hard to follow because nothing really *happened*. It has something to do with the slave trade, and something to do with pirates, and after that it was a popular summer resort with vacation homes and a hotel, *You know, like the Hamptons* (right . . .), until it fell out of fashion in the twenties.

Swan is one of ten islands in a little archipelago called the Shoals, ten miles off the coast of New Hampshire. There's a marine research center on Duck; people have retreats and conferences in the summer on Star. There was a poet who lived on Appledore, the island just south of Swan, in the 1800s. Celia Thaxter. I'd never heard of her but it seems like she's famous enough. Tourist boats make trips through the Shoals most days in the summer and they always get off on Appledore (I didn't mean that to be a pun or a *double entendre* or whatever, but they do, I guess) and check out Celia Thaxter's garden.

I went over there once with Lolly. It was one of those days when March pretends it's summer, only to kick your ass with freezing rain two days later. She was worried that I was getting depressed and said that I needed to get some air and exercise, so we got a lift in Ted's boat—he rows people over when they need to smuggle stuff or themselves back to the mainland—and walked around Celia Thaxter's garden. Lolly asked what I thought about it. I said it was nice. She was clearly disappointed that I didn't start skipping through the crocuses and humming a little tune and chasing little Disney chipmunks and blue birds and bunnies. Maybe it wouldn't have killed me to put on more of a show. Celia Thaxter's garden looked exactly like a picture of Celia Thaxter's garden, so it really wasn't necessary to force me into a boat and drag me over a body of water to check out something that was obviously just going to disappoint us both in the end.

We didn't talk when we got home. She went to her room and didn't come out. I cooked something and made a salad with some red and yellow nasturtiums on top—like a peace offering. It was really pretty. But when I yelled up to her she just called back and said she wasn't hungry. And neither was I, really, so when I got sick of just sitting alone at the table I packed everything up and cleaned the kitchen till it was totally spotless and went to bed before it was even dark. And now Lolly's dead and it would have been so easy to make a little bit of an effort when she took me to Appledore. It doesn't matter, but I can't stop thinking about it. I never thought my sparkling personality would be a miracle drug, but maybe it would have made a difference or something. Never mind.

But I was talking about the houses on Swan. Most of them look like Lolly's house—old, white with gray roofs, wooden and straight and, I don't know, really house-shaped, like the picture of a house you'd draw if you were a kid who was really good at drawing. But there are a couple of exceptions. Some people have gone all out. Marie is a widow in her eighties who's made her house look exactly like it belongs to a witch in a story. It's short and purple and surrounded by wildflowers and grasses taller than I am. The air around it is thick with bees and butterflies and whatever she's got on the stereo. Jefferson Airplane or Fleetwood Mac. She dresses to match her house in long skirts and lots of jewelry that looks like it performs some kind of magical function, sucking up moonlight to save for later, or hiding poison or medicine or blades. The kind of thing my mom likes to wear. Marie calls herself the Island Crone, but actually a lot of people call themselves that, so many that I had to go and look up what it meant.

The Psychedelicatessen is another building that stands out. It's the island's only café, run by a husband-and-wife team, Suzie Q and Johnny Come Lately. They seem to know how weird they are, which is comforting and funny because otherwise they would be pretty scary. They wear matching leather jackets with *Hell's Angels* written across the back, even when it's way too hot. Their motorcycles are two of the only vehicles on the island, along with some mopeds and three or four golf carts. I don't know if electric wheelchairs count. The Psychedeli looks just like the name sounds, like a tie-dyed shirt with skeletons wearing top hats and *Come on inside for a little touch of grey* . . . graffitied underneath. The couple next door helps them when they get really busy—Helen and Nancy, who are only sixty-six and sixty-seven. People under seventy are usually called "youngsters" here, which got more complicated when I arrived, 'cause some people started calling me "the youngster" and then people got confused about whether someone was talking about *a* youngster or *the* youngster, but it's not such a huge problem that we have to call the Coast Guard or anything and we have plenty of free time here, so sometimes it gives you something to talk about.

A bunch of Swans are doing tai chi outside the chapel. They really do look like birds when they do it. When I manage to leave the house on time in the morning I like to stop and watch them. Secretly, I'd like to join in, but the Swans usually don't like it when I join things. Today there's no time to stop, but I slow my pace a little. I like the dinky Quaker chapel. It's compact, made of white stone and wood. It doesn't think it's the shit like big cathedrals do. The chapel's just another house, really. The only thing that sets it apart is the one tower, square like a chimney but taller than any of the others, with a big iron bell hanging inside.

God, I really want to stop today, watch for a while, go into the chapel and sit in the pews and think, or maybe ring the bell a couple of times. Something about this morning is starting to sting. A few minutes with Rose will help. The pie gives me an excuse to pop in.

Rose has little chimes above the door that tinkle gently when you walk in. It's a nice touch.

Rose lifts her warm, walnut face from her accounting book. "Hi, Sugar!"

"Hi, Rose. Brought you something."

Her hands slide against mine, just for a moment, soft and cool and comforting, as she takes the pan from me. Rose pulls back the dishcloth and takes a whiff before she pulls off a pinch with her thumb and forefinger and munches away. "A little stingy with the cinnamon, but the crust ain't half bad. Must be them cold hands you got. Cold hands make the best pastry."

She likes my pie; the relief is almost painful.

"Nice boots," I offer, not ready to leave yet.

"Good, eh? My niece sent 'em from the Bad Place with a tourist and Ted rowed them over from Appledore."

The Bad Place is where we all come from. Some people think it's nasty to call it that. Mostly it's referred to as *the mainland* or *off-island* but some people are adamant. They left for a reason and they aren't going back except maybe in a mahogany box. Rose says she wants to be dropped in the sea, that she'd rather be fish food than go back there. She's really sweet, I don't want to give you the impression that she's hateful and twisted, but she is a bit fucked up and she'll admit it. She was raped by two teenage boys when she was sixty. She's seventy-two now. They followed her home; it was still light out. One of them held her down while the other one raped her. And then they switched. She said she screamed the whole time but apparently no one heard, which is fucking typical. She still limps on account of they fractured her hip. She said it helps to talk about it, and that that night is the reason she came to Swan. She needed a place to be old where she'd be safe and where she could be herself. I told her I hated people who did that, preyed on the weak. She looked angry and said, "I am *not* weak." And I said I didn't mean her. I think she understood. So I guess it's fair to say that me and Rose are pretty close.

But anyway, her new boots are like knee-high moccasins with fringes and turquoise beads. With her brown legs and denim mini-skirt she looks like that Native American princess. She even has her long gray hair in two braids to match. She once told me that she used to dress like Mother Teresa on her day off, but that all changed once she moved out to Swan.

"They're great. You look like that Native American princess."

She laughs that big, chicken-and-dumplings laugh of hers. "*Pocahontas*, you little ignoramus. Shouldn't you be at school?"

"Mental-health day."

That's our little joke.

"Well, Miss Mental Health Day, you better move that caboose. You're late."

I am, or nearly anyway.

Before I can make an excuse, Rose starts shaking her head and clears her throat. "Got a call from Nick a minute ago," she says with deliberate lightness, like someone calling a hurricane a spell of windy weather. "Says the slip last night rumbled the cat awake and it went skittering across his bed. Everything all right down at Violet's?"

I don't miss a beat. "It's fine. I didn't notice anything last night. Slept like a baby."

This makes Rose roll her eyes. I wish I could remember not to say stupid shit like that.

"You know I don't like you in that house," she says flatly.

"No one likes me in that house."

"And that'll do with the back talk."

"Sorry, Rose." Just before I say goodbye, I build the courage to put myself in the way of disappointment. "By the way, when Ted brought over the boots from your niece, was there any mail for me, like bills or whatever?"

"Nothing for you, sugar." She does that head-tilt thing that people do when they're trying to be affectionate or sympathetic, but when Rose does it, it doesn't seem fake. It doesn't make me feel better, though. It's like, come on, if they're not going to call, they could write me a letter, send a postcard. Even if they couldn't remember where they'd written down the address, even if they couldn't even remember my name, they could just write: *The Kid, Swan Island, New Hampshire* and it would have gotten to me.

"He did bring a stack of newspapers, not even that old."

"Just a paper then, Rose."

I slide my nickel across the counter and she pulls a copy of the *New York Times* from two days ago out from under it and drops it down with a satisfying slap. That's just the way she likes to do things, like everything needs a big *yee-haw* at the end. I know that five cents is cheap for a newspaper. The community subsidizes the price for nostalgic value so it only costs a nickel. This fat, ridiculous coin that's pretty much good for nothing. Even pennies make up odd amounts, so they're useful even if they're practically worthless. On Swan Island selling newspapers makes a loss because the newspapers cost a nickel and that's the way they like it.

"Go on now, scoot." She turns away to switch on the radio—she likes Top 40s in the morning—and I catch her limping as she goes to take a box down from a far shelf. The little bells jingle behind me, laughing at a private joke.

Next to Rose's grocery is the Relic, Swan's tavern, then a rocky hill I have to climb up to get to Mrs. Tyburn's house. The Relic is full every night and plays on the whole pirate island thing, the way that Bluebeard or Blackbeard or one of those dudes was supposed to have spent some time here, marauding or hiding treasure or whatever. I forget. It has one of those cute signs out front that swings from a chain old-fashioned-style with a picture of a ship on it. The blackboard outside always says the same thing:

Abandon all hope, ye who enter here.
Eat, Drink, and Be Merry
For Tomorrow We Die!

Another thing about this place is that the island is so small that you can see the ocean from wherever you are, which I really could do without. Seeing all that water is when it comes back to me: Lolly and my parents are gone, and however nice Rose and Suzie and Johnny are, I'm alone.

But the Swans are really proud of being able to always see the ocean. I've had at least four of them corner me at one point or another and whisper, like it's the most amazing secret ever, "Have you noticed that you can see the ocean from every point on the island?" And I play dumb every time and say something like, "Wow, that's amazing," and then look around and say, "Oh, yeah, I see what you mean. Wow." Older people really need you to put on a little show for them sometimes. It's annoying.

The terrain flattens out to the last stretch leading up to Mrs. Tyburn's house. Hers is taller and broader than most of the others, the same age as the chapel and the Oceanic, with fancy gables perched on top like a tiara. It's just before nine when I let myself in. Mrs. Tyburn's the only person I know with those long, old-fashioned keys, the kind that jailers have in old movies. And, as far as I know, the only one who bothers to lock her door on Swan. Even though I've done this a hundred times I'm still nervous when I walk through the foyer over floorboards dark and serious enough to be part of a musical instrument. The huge portrait of her late husband hangs on the far wall. It's one of the parts of this job I'm looking forward to the least. I can doctor vacation snapshots and tweak home movies, but I'm not sure my skills will stretch to cinching the waist of a large man in an oil painting. I'll do what I always do. Break life up into its parts, make it soft, blow it up, and fix it a pixel at a time.

CHAPTER TWO

I spend three days a week editing Mrs. Tyburn's life. No anxiety here about becoming a youth-unemployment statistic; there's plenty to do. Boxes of photographs and slides, dozens of hours of 8 mm films. Letters, diaries, insurance inventories, wills, deeds.

I go through to her kitchen, bigger and brighter than the last few apartments I lived in with my parents, light the stove, put on the kettle, and drop two bags of Earl Grey into the porcelain pot with the violets on the side. The grandfather clock chimes in the hall. In moments like this, when it's quiet and I'm surrounded by her Victorian array of specialist dishes and utensils that have only one very particular use—the olive pitter, the grape shears, the tiny saw for slicing lemons, the silver sugar tongs—I know that this job could go on forever. And then I start to wonder if maybe she'll just die soon and let me off the hook.

But I know there's no use dwelling on it. I've agreed to it, to go through every frame of her life and adjust it to her satisfaction. And maybe then I'll have my own life. Maybe I'll be able to take six months and trek through the Andes, climb pyramids, sit in an arroyo in the desert and sing with the coyotes.

"What an interesting skirt. Is it new?"

I spill some hot water onto the counter as Mrs. Tyburn enters. She tuts at my clumsiness through dust-pink lips. Her hair is pinned into the sort of intricate knot that you only see in old pictures. She's finally managed to find a color of pale blond that recedes easily into her white roots without jarring the eye. She's tiny, as if age takes a little piece off her body as the minutes go by. She doesn't have the droopy bottom and boobs some women get in menopause. She's just compacted, like she's shrinking to death.

Somehow, though, I always feel smaller when I'm with her, like her kind of aging is contagious. It makes me uneasy.

"Yes, it's new. I mean, new to me at least. Do you like it?"

Her expression doesn't change. "Red."

Charcoal slacks, black boat-neck top, pearls. I shrink and feel that I have to really reach to take down the cups and saucers. She takes a pair of reading glasses out of the drawer that holds the notepads, pens, and the ten-year-old phone book. The pearls of the chain on her glasses match her necklace exactly. I take my notebook out of my bag and turn to the most recent page.

"So, where were we?" she asks.

"Sophia's diary, June eighteenth, 1977."

"Oh, yes. Read back the last paragraph."

"'Today is Jenny's birthday. She's my best friend at camp because she's pretty and kind and she let me have the top bunk. I said we could swap every two days so that we could both have the top bunk.'"

"Put an exclamation point there. No, two exclamation points. She was fond of overpunctuating as a child."

"'We both got care packages from home today, but the one from my mom was the biggest out of anyone in my cabin. I think the other girls were jealous, so I put the raisins and peanuts out on the card table for everyone to share. I have to remember to wrap them up again before lights out so we don't get ants. Mommy also sent me the new Nancy Drew mystery—I'm already finished with the first chapter. When I'm done I'll see if Martha will trade it for one of her Famous Five books from England.'"

"Excellent work, my girl. Sounds exactly like her at her best. I always said that she really thrived when she was able to mobilize her resilience and the resourcefulness she inherited from her father and me." She leans in closer to check the handwriting in my draft against the original. On that day in 1977, little Sophia actually confessed to stealing all of her bunkmate's chocolate. She'd snuck in during craft time, and even though she had plenty of chocolate from her mother's care packages she'd torn through the other girl's stash and buried the wrappers in the woods. When the theft was discovered, she denied it, confessing only to her antacid-pink diary with *Secrets* in cursive across the cover and a supremely pathetic lock. At least I've already finished rewriting her letters, a poor kid begging her mother to let her come home.

Mrs. Tyburn thinks "Sophia's" handwriting should be smaller and more rounded when I transcribe the alternative story into the replica diary. Piece of cake.

"Very nearly perfect," she says. "Leave the rest with me and I'll be up soon with my corrections. Finish up the diary and after that make a start at slimming her down in the pictures. The group photos might be a bit tricky because that silly Instamatic camera she had was dreadful, but I know you'll work your usual magic. And if you have time, perhaps you'll make a start at fixing that boat." She means the pictures of the boat.

With this she curls her fingers—which are somehow both skeletal and amazingly soft—around my chin, beaming pride at me. The truth is that I'm her favorite child because I've fallen for her only trick like neither of her real children ever would. I need her money, I rely on it, so during billable hours I'll do and say just about anything she wants. I'm hers like no one else has ever been.

The phone rings sharp through the halls of the house, threatening to shatter the glass cabinet fronts and all the fancy tchotchkes behind them, but she's still got her talons clamped to my jaw and doesn't let me go until she purrs, "That must be Ted running early with the prints. Keep your seat—I'll speak to him."

Her breast brushes my shoulder when she reaches for the phone. I think about teddy bears—the soft ones that little kids take to bed and the hard ones that grown-up women collect. Mrs. Tyburn has the second kind.

While we finish our tea Mrs. Tyburn gives me a few more notes. As she talks, new things occur to her, dozens of details to make her daughter's childhood happier, so many that I have to ask her to slow down.

"I suppose they don't teach young women shorthand anymore. This must be difficult for you."

Last of all, for the time being at least, I have to deal with Sophia's clothes. Mrs. Tyburn wants her daughter to wear "brighter colors" (which means more pink), and finds it odd that she wore corduroys when it was obviously too hot. (I tug my sweaty bra line and see her point.) Is there anything I can do about this? Of course, I tell her. That's what I always say. Nothing she asks is impossible. I clear up and take my notes to the impromptu edit suite she has set up for me in her attic. I like to pretend I'm that character from *A Little Princess*, working away with a beacon of optimism keeping me going: the storybook knowledge that my daddy will return from whatever war that was, shake off his amnesia, and come for me.

This room is different from the rest of the house, where everything looks one-of-a-kind and carefully made. The attic makes me feel rejected, like she doesn't really want me in her house. But there's nowhere else to put me. Story of my life. In here the furniture is new and cheap. The L-shaped desk and the adjustable office chair are from Ikea and could sit in any room, anywhere. The plastic-wood drawers have plastic-metal handles. There's no inkwell carved into dark wood or little decorative things with tiny clockworks that jingle and bing for no reason.

I shouldn't complain, though—I didn't expect her to go out antiquing for me when she hired me to digitize her family archive, and she topped up her old equipment with everything I said I'd need for the job. I have a great computer with two big screens for editing, all the most up-to-date software, a brand-new scanner, and a photo-quality printer as well as an inkjet one for ordinary documents. And then there's the old photo equipment, the ancient slide carousel, the two-reel projector, the eight-track player, two typewriters. (I jot a note on a Post-it that one is almost out of ribbon.) Even the Betamax video player in orange-and-beige faded plastic and the clunky black audiocassette player have a certain charm. I pull up my chair and press the on buttons, listen to the fizzle and crack of the machines waking up. I log in and check my email; yeah, I didn't expect anything to have come through from my folks since I left the house. It doesn't matter.

Mrs. Tyburn thinks I'm some kind of genius. I feed myself with her mistake. It's a good thing I have the place to myself up here. I spend most of my time googling error messages and watching online tutorials and asking questions on forums about how to do this or that in Photoshop, winging it, hitting undo a hundred times until I manage. I'm not bad at most things now, but when I started I didn't have a fucking clue.

———

Mrs. Tyburn and I met on a First Friday just after I arrived last January. First Fridays are when they let visitors onto Swan. Some of the Wrinklies want it to be less often than that, the hard-line separatists, like Nick. I wish they could just be patient. I didn't ask to exist, and I certainly didn't ask to exist here. It's just shit luck. My mom had my full astrological chart read once. The guy kept talking about *hard lessons* and *learning experiences* and I could tell he was really saying, "Sorry, kiddo; your life is going to be shit." My mother was always getting me stuff I didn't need for my birthday, stupid trinkets or experiences she thought would be, like, groovy, when I really could have used the cash.

That particular Friday, when I met Mrs. Tyburn, was clear and not too cold, so there were lots of families out playing games or eating and chatting on blankets in the grass. My parents didn't come, of course; I'd asked Lolly to invite them and she'd agreed, but later she said the two numbers they'd left—a cell and a landline—

had both been disconnected. So I was walking by on my way to visit the Duchess and to get something for lunch from Rose's shop, and Mrs. Tyburn was out with little clusters of people, directing a middle-aged couple and their pimply teenage son to pose with the sea in the background. It was a good picture—puffy clouds on a bright blue sky and a breeze wrapping the woman's green dress around her shins. The woman's beige coat and tan scarf were so neat and crisp they could have been made of origami.

"No, stay just like that," Mrs. Tyburn urged them. "Don't move, I'll get it."

"Oh, Mother, please," said the woman.

Then the man said, "Let me have a look."

"No, no, stay right where you are. It's perfect, just like that. I'll get the . . . I'll get this . . . this . . . damned thing . . ."

As if she could feel me watching, Mrs. Tyburn turned and called me over. Obviously, she knew who I was, but in my first few weeks I'd managed to avoid her. "You young people know how to get these things working, don't you? For the money I paid for it, it could at least do me the service of taking a simple snapshot, don't you think?"

She had it set to video. Plus the lens cap was on.

Once she'd taken four or five shots of the family, they walked off, the woman huffing and mumbling to her husband. Mrs. Tyburn ignored them while I showed her how to see the photos she'd just taken and how to delete the ones she didn't like. She complained that she couldn't see the boy's face well enough in one shot and I said that she could use a computer program to change the contrast and get rid of some of the shadow.

"My, youth today. Such technical expertise." I wanted to walk away but I could tell she had something more to say, and I had to wait while she worked out exactly what. "You know, I have a veritable library of images that could use a touch-up like this, and my son-in-law says that all of my pictures really should go onto compact discs. My dear, your particular brand of savvy could be just what this old woman needs. I think five dollars an hour would be suitable. Yes."

I started to accept before I realized it wasn't actually a question.

———

An updated version of InDesign shoves its new features onto my screen with a pop-up sporting an image of a bird whose acid-trip tail brags about their clever design chops (so, if I take the virtual tour, I'll be able to design a similarly magnificent creature!). It's the kind of window you feel like you have to deal with because the option to *skip this step* is tiny and faint, a dweeby kid cowering in a corner of the window. So I bite and click through the whole intro-tour of the updated interface until Mrs. Tyburn comes in with her revisions to Sophia's diary, much of it just squiggles and symbols and shorthand, and goes out again to a more charming part of the house. Mostly I understand what the symbols mean from context. But there's one I have to look up. *Stet*, verb—let it stand. In a proof a revision that should be ignored, like crossing out a crossing out. Let it remain. *Stet, stet.* I like it. It hits hard enough to hurt a little but not too bad. It makes an impact.

I look at more of the search hits and find out that there's a book called *Stet* by some lady who used to be a book editor, and I consider ordering it, but that'll take a month and I'll be gone by then for sure. I wonder if it means the same thing to her that it means to me, if it's one of those really sad words for her too. Of course she edited books and I edit some old lady's fucked-up life. Still, I imagine reading it and emailing her to tell her what I think. Maybe she'd write me back. I have really stupid ideas sometimes.

Stet. The more I repeat it in my head, the more desperate it makes me feel. I can't stop saying it, though. Let it remain. Like a prayer, short and kind of pathetic, because it doesn't matter what you say or do; whatever's going to happen is going to happen no matter what. There's no magic. That's what made me feel so shitty about it, this *stet*. Mrs. Tyburn can get me to fix her life and change her family and make it look like everybody loves her because she has the money to pay me to do it. But I can't do it for myself, my family, my life. I'll say *stet* when things feel really awful, if only to be cruel to myself. Stet, I say, I ask, I beg. Only, I'll never be able to instruct like she does. I'll never be able to make anything stay.

An hour or so later, the doorbell rings. Even though I'm all the way at the top of the house, it's up to me to answer it. Only respectful, I guess. It's Ted with the pictures. He has this rickshaw-style bike he uses to deliver stuff to the Swans. He was a graphic designer before he retired, which is handy when I'm really stuck with something, though I try not to bother him too much. Mrs. Tyburn actually asked him first to do my job, but he said it sounded way more complicated than anything he was into now. I think he also realized that the job was going to be creepy as hell and didn't want to be part of it.

"Hey, kid," he huffs as he lifts one of the larger pictures out of the trailer behind his bike. "Seven framed portraits, for Her Majesty's approval. Nice job on the color and shade around the faces. Your work is really coming along." Ted's the only one who can really see what I do.

"Thanks. And thanks for bringing them over. Do you want to come in for a cup of coffee or anything? I could show you how I've set up the projections to transfer the home movies to digital."

A drop of sweat slides down from his wispy white hairline and soaks into his eyebrow. "I'll take a rain check." And he takes the envelope from Mrs. Tyburn that I hand him. "Hey, don't work too hard up there." He mounts his stocky frame on his bike and rides away the long way where the path is smoother and the slope longer and less steep.

There's something bothering me as I bring the pictures inside. I'm in an awkward position as I shift each picture inside while keeping the door from swinging closed with my foot. But that's not it. It takes a second before I recognize the feeling. Anxiety is like a bad joke you've heard before. It comes up with this ridiculous energy, but it's really the same boring shit as ever. I'm anxious about what will happen if Mrs. Tyburn doesn't like the photos, or if I've offended her in some other way, or if she's gotten tired of me. I've hardly managed to save anything yet, and if she fired me, that would be that. I still wouldn't know where my parents were. I wouldn't be able to keep the lights on or the phone connected. And eventually I'd have to find Ted—probably tinkering in his tool shed, or at the Psychedeli playing guitar with Johnny, or in the Relic, doing whatever they do in there—and ask him to row me over to Appledore. We'd head to the pier, me clutching my bag and avoiding the concerned, encouraging eyes of the Wrinklies. I'd sit in the sun in Celia Thaxter's boring garden and watch the beads of sweat form on my folded arms and drip into the dirt, heave my bones onto the next boat back to the Bad Place, alone. I'd probably end up just like my folks, wherever they are. Except I'm alone and at least they have each other.

"Bring them through, darling! Oh, it's just like Christmas!"

I take the pictures into the kitchen one at a time. Mrs. Tyburn reaches into her drawer and pulls out a little pair of scissors, the one she uses to open boxes, packages, and envelopes with that new kind of adhesive she hates. By the time I come through with the third one she's staring at the first, unwrapped on the kitchen table. She pulls off her glasses and lets them bounce against her breasts.

"You, my girl, are an absolute prodigy." The portrait of her son—with creamy, boyish skin instead of an angry rash of teenage acne—looks up at me as if he doesn't entirely agree.

"My *darling* girl! How perfect, how marvelously perfect! Now, quickly with the others. I cannot *wait*."

In the picture of her high school graduating class, the tassel on her cap now has the same stripes as the kids who'd graduated with honors. She fills out her gown with polite, round B cups and she has *two* perfectly shaped eyebrows. In the shot of her in a bikini with her college girlfriends she has grown into a C. It's a sunny day now, and the palm trees actually have banana leaves because she didn't like the ones that were there on the day. Too brown, too fan-like; the banana shape is more to her taste. Her friend Michelle's front teeth are the same length and that "dreadful portly child" in the background has vanished, along with the "flaccid excuse for a castle" he'd been building. Midway through her degree, fully developed into ample, high-set Ds, she and Herbert Tyburn pose in front of a dance-contest trophy. "Let's make it second place. And change it to the Lindy Hop. Foxtrot sounds so stuffy these days, don't you think?" And on through the years, births, milestones, candid moments. I've given her real breasts, grateful children, a husband whose eyes never wandered. In these seven pictures, that is. There are still boxes and boxes of A cups to enhance, frowns to invert, people to insert or delete, an upper lip to paste onto her husband every memorable day for fifty years. I double-check and she assures me she's happy with the prints, so the next time she's out I'll gather up the originals and destroy them.

————

At a little past one, I decide to take my lunch break. This is one of those awkward moments when I feel like I'm taking forever to make a really boring decision. I could go to the Psychedeli (and return some tapes Johnny lent me), but I'm saving up for when my parents call and tell me to come and meet them wherever they've ended up. So I should make something, but there's no food in the house. I'd have to buy something from Rose and take it back and fix it at home, which would take most of my break. I could just work through lunch but Mrs. Tyburn doesn't pay me extra. I tried it once, when I gave her my hours for the week. But instead of paying me an extra fifteen dollars, she said that that's not what we'd agreed to and anyway she wasn't going to incentivize workaholism, which is a bad habit and I'm at just the age when you should guard against bad habits. She said it all in this really confident way, like she'd noticed me working through lunch all week and had prepared her speech in advance. I guess that's how rich people get that way; they know how to avoid giving money away. She lifted her chin and kind of half raised her eyebrows, but didn't look at me. Her eyes were pointed down like she was really talking to her ridiculous fake boobs.

Plus it's a nice day. Being cooped up in here too long can get me down.

I'm not really hungry anyway, so I go to the Oceanic to see the Duchess. The Oceanic used to be a hotel, back when people would come out to the Shoals on vacation, before World War One or something. A couple of retired doctors and three retired nurses live here along with six Swans who might be in nursing homes if they still lived on the mainland. Johnny and Suzie Q call it Stairway to Heaven. It's small for a hotel, and it's peaceful; the lawn tilts slowly downward and the grass recedes until it becomes a thick forehead of beach. Some red-bottomed rowboats are stacked upside down next to a big coil of rope. It's like a picture; it's really pretty and it feels like I'm not actually here. This is where Lolly died.

Everyone at the Oceanic can get around on their own; they just need someone close, just in case. Except the Duchess. She has Alzheimer's and it's gotten bad. It was already pretty awful when I got here six months ago. She thought I was the daughter of the maid she had when she was a kid. I walked past the porch one day—the Oceanic has this big porch that wraps all the way around three sides of the building, super-broad with lots of rocking chairs, so the Swans can rock and stare at the sea. Anyway, I was walking past and she called out to one of the nurses, "There's my friend.

Mabel's little girl. She comes to play with me." So I came up and sat next to her and let her talk. She asked me questions, too, but she didn't always understand the answers. Sometimes she just smiled and looked out at the waves; sometimes she corrected me. Like when she asked what grade I was in and I told her that I didn't go to school anymore, but I should be a senior, she went, "No, that's not right. You're in the same grade as me, but you go to the Negro school." And I'm thinking, wow, you're fucking *old*.

I kind of played along after that, like a game of let's pretend whose rules I had to keep guessing at. I asked her what her teacher's name was and which girls she played with. Eventually I came up with some really great stuff, like asking her if she had a TV (I even called it a *television set*, really old-fashioned because as far as she was concerned, on that day at least, both of us were ten and it was nineteen-forty-something). And she knew all the answers to everything I asked. She told me how her teacher wore her hair— parted on the side with her bangs swept over her forehead and pinned onto her temple, with the rest braided into a complicated bun at the base of her skull—and that she'd wear it the same way when she grew up. She told me that Jimmy O'Malley would bring a cigarette he'd taken from his mother's purse and smoke it after school. The girls all thought he was disgusting because stealing is a sin and you shouldn't smoke until you're in high school. I asked what she thought of the moon landing and she giggled and said she thought only boys read space comics.

On the day I met her she was wearing a pink dress with burgundy flowers on it. And her hair was just like she described her teacher's. Except that her teacher's hair was golden and the Duchess's was silver.

She makes me want to remember things, which isn't always nice, to be honest, but it feels like the right thing to do. It feels like the only thing I can do for her.

After a couple of months she changed, though, and it was a toss-up whether she'd be happy to see me—smiling or doing this giggle that made me think of gingerbread, I don't know why. Or whether she'd be terrified, convinced I'd come to steal things from her. She'd cry and wail and throw things at me until I left. Or whether she'd ignore me completely.

On good days we would go for walks or sit together on the porch of the Oceanic. She had this funny habit where she made wishes over everything. If a red bird flew by or a boat went past. Sunsets, rainbows, if I stumbled over the doorjamb of the entryway. Her wishes were always different—good weather tomorrow, someone to bring her treats, health for someone in her family, for her baby sister to go to heaven or for her baby sister to come back (she died of tuberculosis when she was six and the Duchess was eight), for the war to end. Mine was always the same until one day she asked, "Is that really what you want?" I told her it was what I *needed*, and so what was the point bothering God or the universe or whatever for anything else?

"But what do you *want*? You must want something, even some little thing?" I thought about the world, the future. Beached whales, people in surgical masks walking along highways bathed in smog, tap water you can set on fire. Waiting in line outside a football stadium with my folks for someone to look at our teeth, waiting in line outside a church for groceries, waiting here . . . I told her I couldn't think of anything.

"Then you'll never get anything, silly."

"I'm sure it doesn't work like that."

She brushed her fingers across my forehead and the front of my hair. "I wish you could be less afraid. Just a little less. Come 'ere, I have an idea." A grin crinkled up around her dark brown eyes, and she led me up to her room faster than I'd ever seen her move before. Her hand clamped enthusiastically around my wrist was girlishly small.

She led me over to her dresser and pulled a little red change purse out of her top drawer. "Here." She pressed a coin into my palm. "It's a real Indian Head penny. For courage, like a brave."

I was relieved she stopped there and didn't make any embarrassing noises with her hand over her mouth like she did sometimes when she thought we were kids playing.

I was torn between playing along and wanting to avoid her finding it missing and accusing me of having taken it, especially because she would have been half right. "I can't take your lucky penny."

"But aren't we friends?"

"I . . . I have a hole in my pocket. It'll fall out on my way home. Will you keep it safe for me and I'll come back and get it tomorrow?"

I could say that because neither of us really knew what "tomorrow" meant. She beamed at the responsibility.

That night she had the first stroke. Rose told me it wasn't too bad, and when I came to visit I found her sitting up with her eyes open wide, like she was looking at something she couldn't quite believe. Her eyes darted to me in the doorway and followed me as I settled into the chair next to her.

"It's just so sad about the teacher." Her sigh was almost a groan. Her wrinkles all sank downward, like she was disappointed in God.

"Your teacher?"

"I don't know what they wanted to go to space for anyway. Why can't anyone just stay here? Just stay, just stay."

Nothing I said would get through. Helen and Nancy came later and said she must be talking about a space shuttle that had exploded, sometime before I was born. Like she was stuck on that event and couldn't stop reliving it. "What's a school teacher need to go to space for, anyway? Why didn't she just stay here? Just stay . . ."

Her second stroke followed just two days later and the Swans had a meeting in the chapel.

I walk up the big staircase that leads to the porch and the entrance to the Oceanic. It's almost grand, as grand as Shaker buildings can be, I suppose. Lots of space and air and light. The foyer has high ceilings, a wood floor, and white walls that make the room feel comforting instead of sterile. Gretchen comes out of one of the ground-floor rooms, the one they use for checkups and stuff. She's not technically a youngster, but she's only seventy-one. She moved here with a much older guy she was seeing. He died in the Oceanic two years ago. That's what Rose told me, and she knows everything about everyone on Swan.

"All right, lovely? Here to visit the Duchess?"

I nod. "Can I do anything, help with anything?"

As usual, Gretchen considers my offer seriously. She ducks into her office for a moment and comes back with a tiny pair of spring-loaded scissors. "Her nails are getting a bit long. Be *careful*."

"I know." As if I would hurt her. I would never.

The Duchess lives in room sixteen, just at the top of the first flight of stairs. She hasn't done anything for a long time. She can't eat anymore. She can't move. For a while after the second stroke, she'd make sounds, almost words sometimes. Then she'd move her mouth and shake her head like she was trying to wake herself up from a nightmare. Now she doesn't even do that. She made it clear—back when she could still make things clear—that she didn't want to be kept alive in a "vegetative state" and that this is where she wanted to die. The Swans are having a meeting on Sunday to decide how to kill her. Rose says I can't come.

Her room is light. They put her bed by the big window but it's not like she can turn her head to enjoy the view. Some things we do are to make things easier for the person in pain and other things are to make it easier for the people who love them. They always keep fresh flowers in her room, lilacs today. They're really perfume-y and they're making me feel a bit high.

"Hi. It's me. It's my lunch hour." Talking aloud when no one hears you makes everything sound really loud. But it doesn't matter. I put my stuff down at the foot of the bed and take her hands into mine. They're so small and almost brown between the dark spots and the tape that holds her IV needle in place. And so delicate it's almost hard to touch them, like they're made of warm water or glass that's not quite set. There's a flat brown mole on the fleshy part below her right thumb that I never noticed before. I check that no one's in the doorway before I give it a tiny kiss. Then I start clipping.

"It finally stopped raining. It's hot today, hardly any clouds." The clock on the wall clacks. The machine that monitors her heart beeps in horrible syncopation with the clock. The machine that breathes for her sucks and drops, a blue accordion in a tube. The snap of the nail clippers sends sharp crescents flying onto the bedspread or the floor. She's still growing, even now, still doing something all on her own. But it's nothing to get all optimistic about. It doesn't mean anything.

I gather up the clippings and take them to the trash can. On the shelf above it there's a bottle of hand sanitizer that I forgot to use before I cut her nails. We'll just keep this between us. I sit in the chair next to her bed, pick up the book I've been reading to her, and start where I left off yesterday:

When someone sleeps they become a child again, perhaps because in sleep one can do no evil and one is unaware even of one's own existence. By some natural magic, the worst criminal, the most inveterate egoist is made sacred by sleep.

After I've been here for nearly an hour, I stop reading and look at her, lying in bed, existing. Her crocheted beige slippers are still under her bed, even though she'll never use them again. She's going to die very soon.

The clack of the wall clock tears gristle apart. Each beep of the heart monitor shrieks alarm. The machine that breathes for her sucks and drops, a blue accordion in a tube, pulling in hard hope, and giving up.

She has a heart that works, that bleeps the machine and pulls a line across the screen.

Clack, bleep, suck, drop.

I am her brain. I can't tell her race; her skin is worn, brown, seasoned. She could be my grandmother. Her cheekbones are the edge of the cliff. The skin underneath curves in at a dangerous angle, then hollows, soft as soil and brown and ridged and marked. Too much like a skull. Her eyes are closed. Oxygen goes in through the tube taped to her nose. Her mouth open and soundless, letting a draft sweep through the curve of her face.

Clack, bleep, suck, drop.

I am her lost mind.

It's time to go, but it's hard to leave the swim of flower smell and the softness of the Duchess's room, so I read to her, just a little more.

We sleep our lives away, the eternal children of Fate. That's why, if I think with that feeling, I experience an immense, boundless tenderness for all of infantile humanity, for the somnambulist lives people lead, for everyone, for everything.

"Aha!" Gretchen's voice from the doorway stabs the silence. "I've figured out her game. She finds the most depressing book on the island, recites a little every day in that lugubrious tone you can't really strike after adolescence. All us Wrinklies slide into comas as well, and the island's all hers."

Gretchen and Frances, one of the nurses, are giving me little teasing grins. "Quick, Dr. Diaz," Frances gasps. "Take my pulse. I think my will to live is still hanging on by *a thread*."

"We've got your number, junior."

"Devious shit, kid."

If I were holding Storytime, I would have brought juice boxes and rung the bell. Sorry, I don't take requests, but if you don't like what I'm reading you could always try, I don't know, *not* mooching in doorways listening to private conversations like an analogue NSA. You probably expect me to read a bunch of lovely stuff, Celia Thaxter poetry or, like, Wordsworth or Emerson or whatever. Well, fuck that. I'll read what I want.

Of course, I can't say any of this aloud. I talk back and the next thing I know they've told Rose and she's giving me one of her talks about *respect for your elders* and *no one likes a smart-ass* and *you're a guest here, young lady, and your behavior should reflect that*. I'm not *even* a guest. I'm as much of a guest here as a crack baby in a hospital dumpster.

"It's those pesky overactive libidos."

"Thank God that's over."

"Speaking of libidos, what day is it?"

"Why," Frances puts on fake surprise. "I do believe it's Friday. First one of the month, in fact."

"Already? I wonder who Ted will row over *this* month."

I mark my page with the leaf I've been using and gather up my bag, fighting off the massive smile Gretchen and Frances planted there.

I hand the nail scissors back to Gretchen and they let me by.

"Um, thanks." It seems like the polite thing since I don't know what else to say.

"See you tonight," Frances chants after me.

First Friday of the month. I completely forgot. I take out my phone; I put it on silent when I got to the Oceanic. One missed call. Jason.

CHAPTER THREE

t's late, almost quarter past two, and I'm running again, past the clumps of long, pale grass bent from how the wind's always bothering them. It's hot. My underarms are all itchy. I shouldn't be nervous about Jason coming but I can't help it. Little e-fiend butterflies are having a sweaty rave in my stomach as I climb the hill. Jesus, it got really hot. And what am I wearing? It doesn't matter. I don't even look right in my own clothes, so I might as well look wrong in Lolly's. I consider stopping to call Jason back—I'm already late; two more minutes won't make a difference—but I'd rather call when I've gotten my breath back and I'm less at risk of sounding like someone's asthmatic phone stalker.

Mrs. Tyburn is at the kitchen table looking through the Sotheby's catalog. She glances at her watch when I walk in. She won't say anything if I stay a little late tonight.

"Pleasant lunch?"

"Yeah. I went to the Oceanic to read to the Duchess for a bit."

She smiles and sort of coos at me.

Just then her eyes move, and mine follow. Up, then quickly left and right. There's a noise, a long scratch. Now it's gone, and in a second it's back again. When the pitch changes from low to irritatingly high, I can see it. Our eyes meet as it flies between us and then shoot up as it makes for the ceiling. It hovers back down again in a quick zigzag and lands on the edge of the table near the sugar dish. Mrs. Tyburn squints, then moves so fast it makes me flinch.

It's like an igloo exploded—white cubes in the air, scattering across the table and onto the floor. I manage to catch the sugar dish before it falls and shatters. I start picking up the glittering cubes from the tabletop and when Mrs. Tyburn moves the catalog I spot the little body.

"Got it."

Just. She whacked the catalog down when it was on the very edge of the table; it almost got away. Another inch or two and she would have made it. Her wings twitch against the stripy fur on her back.

"Why did you do that?" The words feel cold when they slip out of me.

"It was a bug."

"It was a bee."

Mrs. Tyburn turns her face away from me and kind of scratches her ear. "I suppose they are lovely little furry things."

"Get a hundred more and you can make yourself a coat."

It looks like she's trying to change her facial expression but can't quite make her muscles hit the mark, so I can't tell if she's angry or confused. You're, like, a million years old, I want to say to her. What is Botox supposed to do, make you look half a million?

Because she's my boss, because she's old and I'm not, because

I'd rather face the floor than look at her, because there's a mess now and someone's got to clean it, I go get the dustpan and the tiny broom out from under the sink and sweep her floor.

"Did you manage the rest of the corrections to Sophia's diary?" I nod and try to soften up my face. "Very good. Let's have a look at Herbert's vexing little boat, shall we?"

I hate climbing the stairs with her. It makes me feel like I'm being punished. I like it better when we talk in the kitchen and I'm left to go upstairs on my own and get on with things. It's excruciating, having to walk up three stories at her old lady pace, nothing to say to each other, up to my too-new room in the attic. Plus I'm still pissed off about the bee. You can't kill bees anymore. Everybody knows that. I keep telling myself that one isn't going to make a difference, but instead of making me calmer, I think it's making me more angry—they're fucking endangered, for Christ's sake! The entire goddamn food chain's going to collapse but what does that matter to Grandma Moneybags?

Mrs. Tyburn pulls out an archive box full of film reels, all labeled with strips out of one of those stupid label-making machines, and hands me one marked *July 1975—Our New Yacht, Nantucket*. I thread the leader of the reel into position and guide it through to the take-up reel of her old 8 mm projector, tug down the screen, and pull the blackout curtain.

The first frames are black with dots and blotches. They're always my favorite part, even though they only last a few seconds. Then the scene opens to what looks like a perfect day. The fact that it's in black and white makes it seem even more pristine. The shot pans down from a tasteful scattering of clouds to the masts and sails in a marina. The kids dart into the frame, running but not racing each other. Mr. and Mrs. Tyburn stroll into frame a few beats later. Mrs. Tyburn is a knockout, totally cute in a floral shorts set, full makeup, and a sun hat that blows a little in the wind, forcing her to pose with her hand behind her head. Her breasts barely make an impression. I'm taking notes.

The yacht is smaller than I thought it would be, but I guess my only frame of reference for yachts is rap videos. This one is red and white (the red seems red; it's weird how even in black and white you can kind of tell).

It's called *Jenny*. The name was Mr. Tyburn's idea. Apparently, his mother, Jean, was nicknamed Jenny. *That man's got a nose that grows.* That's what my mother would have said about Mr. Tyburn.

As the family boards the yacht, the attic lights come on. "You get the drift," says Mrs. Tyburn. "We went out on the boat a few times that summer. The name will have to change, and a few minor adjustments will be necessary elsewhere. You do understand?"

"What do you want the boat to be called?"

She does a weird *harrumph* and shrugs really big like she's trying to be flippant when I know she supremely *does* care what the boat is called.

"I mean, naming your yacht after your mother. Is that the done thing, I wonder?" And she actually looks at me, for, like, boat-naming etiquette rules. "Naming your yacht after your sweetheart is far more *de rigueur*. Only, I never did have a nickname, and Maude simply won't do. But you'll think something up, with that magic you do."

She gestures toward my face, nearly touching her fingers to

the underside of my chin, and pulls a long pink smile across her powder-white face.

One night after I'd been working on Mrs. Tyburn's archive for a couple of weeks she called me downstairs. There was a fire burning in the fireplace, and a box of letters beside her. "I'm popping out to see Rose about ordering some things. Would you take care of these? I might be some time; lock up when you're through, will you?" The letters were from someone called Jenny, all addressed to Mr. Tyburn. I only read one or two, enough to be sure they were definitely *not* from his mother.

So now the first thing I've got to do is come up with the nickname she supposedly got from her husband. I decide not to think too hard about it. I Google "yuppie nickname dictionary" and make a list: Topsy, Sooze, Peaches, Mimi, Mitzi, Miffi, Bitsy, Buffy, Bunny. Bunny is a classic, but maybe a bit too stripper these days. Buffy has too many goth connotations, but would Mrs. Tyburn know that? Mimi could work. There's not so much of a leap between Maude and Mimi, but Mimi's also the name of a lady she plays bridge with, and because Mimi always wins Mrs. T is sure she cheats. "Strictly *entre nous*." And then it comes to me, and I know just what to do.

I rewind the film and set up the digital camera on a tripod just below the lens, run a cable from the camera into the computer, and start up Premiere. I set the pixel ratio to 4:3, recording at twenty-four frames per second. The trick to getting the digital copy to look right is to record the image at the same speed it's transmitted. Then I need darkness. I turn off the monitor and cover the standby light with electrical tape, snap the blackout curtains down against the wall so that absolutely no light gets in, wipe the lens super carefully with a special slippery black cloth, flick the light off, and start the film. For the first few seconds it's as dark as it was just before the world started. Just a buzzing noise of something about to happen.

Outside I can hear the grunting roars of walruses that sometimes hang out on the beach up here on the north side of Swan. I'm so anal about anything getting into the room that it makes me jump a little, like the noise is going to break the darkness and ruin the copying process. It takes a second for me to realize the difference between sound and light. My mother liked to hike up here and watch the walruses after Lolly brought us all over, before they ditched me here. We went for a walk together pretty much every day. My mother asked if walruses would eventually evolve out of their blobby shape into something more elegant. I told her that's not how evolution works, which just made us both feel like assholes. She was just making conversation. I didn't need to be mean about it.

We'd been living outside Boston, my parents and me. It was a little communal organic farm in Vermont before that, but my folks got us kicked out. I didn't have to ask why. Work was patchy in Boston and my parents were home a lot, which was the best incentive for me to go to school every day. It wasn't that bad. The other kids let me keep to myself, and I even started to get interested in a couple of subjects, mostly English and French. Eventually a herd of my parents' new friends started coming around, playing guitars and watching TV, smoking tina late into the night, making it impossible for me to sleep. I started missing so much school that I couldn't keep up with the other kids and it was too embarrassing to go. The school sent letters but we all just ignored them until finally Child Services turned up. A teacher had tipped them off when I stopped going to school. As they snooped around the apartment, I kept trying to will the cockroaches to crawl back under the speck-led beige countertops, but they were bolder than ever, like they were trying to get us in trouble. There was a little orange syringe cap on the floor but I don't think they saw it before I kicked it under the couch. We answered their questions on our best behav-ior. My mother spoke to them sweetly about all my problems, in-somnia, trouble concentrating, social anxiety, looking over at me now and then, like she was simply telling them things we talked openly about all the time, some funny, homegrown mystery that had nothing to do with her. My dad rubbed her back or squeezed her shoulder or patted her knee, all sensitive and supportive.

The narcs didn't buy it. The second time they came, they took me with them. My folks were too fucked up to say anything; they stayed in the living room while I packed my stuff. Sometimes I wonder if they noticed at all.

It didn't matter at first. Actually it was a relief; who wants to live in a tiny apartment in the shittiest part of a shitty town with two overgrown teenage junkies? It was actually peaceful, in a way, even with the chaos of the group home, the kids who were just using it as a fucked-up sorority house before they were old enough to be sent to big-girl prison for their thefts and arson and assaults. I knew how to be quiet, and for the most part they left me alone. One of the social workers didn't, but I figured him out quickly enough. He had these stubby hands like lumps of putty with crusty red scabs where he chewed his fingers. I started pretending that I liked it and he lost interest. I went to school on most days and visited my parents for a bit in the afternoon, even though I wasn't technically allowed to go over there. I cleaned up a little, gave them money when I had any. We tried not to make a big deal about it.

In the group home, there was always someone watching you, monitoring, compiling reports, keeping track of your "progress" in a file. There was a camera above every door and one in the common room. If you were in the bathroom too long, pretty soon someone would knock. There was always someone looking at you, but this weirdly constant gaze would always look away long enough to let bad things happen from time to time. I started to notice cameras in town, outside shopping centers and in parking lots, and I felt, not really paranoid, just annoyed, I guess. I had a sense of being looked at all the time, someone watching and waiting for you to do something wrong. Looking at you instead of looking out for you.

Our family court date rolled around, and I was surprised to see that Lolly was there waiting for us. She was early; my parents were forty minutes late. We hugged, and she held me like I'd survived some kind of natural disaster. After the moment passed, though, we had nothing to say to each other. I hadn't really grown since she'd last seen me two years earlier, and she knew it was pointless to ask me about school, so the two go-to subjects for adult-child conversation were DOA. Waiting on the hard bench outside the courtroom, I broke the ice. I took out the book I was reading and told her about it. She'd read it when it came out in the seventies, and asked if I'd gotten to her favorite part, where the narrator freaks out her parents by dismembering the blond baby doll they got her for Christmas. I said I had, and that I loved that part, too. I wanted her to tell me what the funny names of the three prostitutes meant ("China" and "Poland" I could probably have figured out on my own, but "the Maginot Line" confounded my best theories). But she said she didn't know; she just reads for pleasure. I knew I was missing something in that statement—I mean, why else do people read novels?—but I didn't push it, and she seemed happy to sit quietly after that.

Lolly had prepared this stack of research and evidence organized in a neat new folder, bound with elastic and labeled with different-colored tabs and Post-its. Everything she needed, and not a page more. She'd copied transcripts of cases from the past ten years that had any similarity to ours, highlighted passages, composed transitions so one followed another until they formed an airtight case for family intervention instead of making me a super-temporary ward of the state, since I wouldn't be a minor for too much longer. The judge didn't even seem bored while she was talking, and actually sat up straight when she told him how much the county would save if they gave her custody instead of keeping me locked up in the prison for kids with bad taste in parents. Everyone's a winner.

We left for Swan that same week, and she let my parents come with us, even though she was pushing her luck bringing two more youngsters to Swan along with me. I'll never forget that. Help you get settled in, she said. No one talked much in the cab to the ferry in Portsmouth. At the water my legs felt like Popsicles, crunching and threatening to crumble as I forced myself on board. Orange plastic seats with their silly bowl shape making me shift and slide as the boat rocked, too fucking cruel and stupid; I just needed so badly to feel steady. So I held my mother while we crossed. I held her bones. My dad mostly stood out on deck and smoked. Menthols, always menthols.

The weird thing was, there was this big stack of mattresses on the deck. I figured out later that they were for the hotel on Star. The Star Island hippie kids kept trying to climb on top of the stack, and they laughed at each other as each one clawed their way up and rolled off as soon as the boat went over a swell or turned sharply. None of them managed to stay on. And I wanted to try. It was dumb, of course, but I wanted to play too, and I felt like I could have done better, like I could have stayed up there. But *I* wasn't them—I wasn't one of the Star Island kids. I wasn't anybody. I just held my mom and watched my dad smoke and swallowed the feeling that those kids had fucking everything just because none of them looked like their life was ending. I wonder what Lolly did. I can't see her at all now, as hard as I try.

My parents stayed longer than I'd expected, almost two weeks. I could see Lolly losing patience with them, coming home every day and finding them still there, eating her food and doing nothing much with their time. I don't remember them saying goodbye to me either. They must have, though. Right? I remember telling Lolly that I didn't want to go with them to the dock, where Ted was waiting to row them over to Appledore. I walked up to the top of the hill, where the path meets the road, and watched them walk north with this raw ache behind my eyes and nose and in my chest, like when you realize you're coming down with the flu. Mom stuck her hand out and waved. She wore the brave smile of someone being shipped out in the draft.

———

The last frames of the film are just patterns on black, the background flashing fast like a distress call in Morse code, followed by the *tap tap tap* of the end of the reel knocking against the projector with every revolution. I paid attention to most of it. The four of them on their red-and-white boat, having a picnic, Sophia playing with jacks, Mr. T and six-year-old Ben fishing off the side, Mrs. T sunbathing in a floral-patterned bikini top that I'm going to have to fuck around with in Illustrator for ages.

I flip the lights, switch off the projector and camera, roll the mouse, and get started.

I do the stupid boobs first. I'm pretty good at this now—it's really a matter of playing with circles and half spheres. It's the pattern and the shading, and getting them to move fluidly from frame to frame, that's the challenge. She turns around for thirteen seconds. I clip this part out and play with it in a second file. Thirteen seconds, three hundred and twelve frames. Three hundred and twelve frames that I'm pretty much ruining. I mean, what a cutie. I almost feel bad doing it until I realize that a) she's paying me to do it, b) no one else is going to pay me to do anything, c) it's not like I'm actually giving anyone fake boobs, just making the fake boobs she already has a bit more real by letting her pretend that the swollen bulbs she hauls around all day in Bloomingdale's ivory bras were always that way, and that some failure of gravity keeps them floating just south of her chin (they're higher than mine, and I'm a teenager, for Christ's sake), and d) no one is ever going to watch these films anyway.

The digital copy looks pretty good. There are places where it jitters, which makes me uneasy. The edges of objects in the foreground seem almost overdrawn, like the outlines of a cartoon, while in the background the horizon is vague. But not bad, really. It's called generation loss—you inevitably get some when you transfer analog to digital. All you can do is be careful with the aspect ratio and the recording speed. You never transmit in exactly the way you receive—the playback is always different. But that's life. And with all my tampering, what's a little generation loss?

Doing Sophia stings a little. I have a stock photo of her I use as a guide, from the first time I fixed her to Mrs. Tyburn's approval. Opening these frames in Illustrator, I change the brush size to one hundred and liquefy her little sepia legs, use the pucker tool until they're sticks with some prepubescent hint of a shape. I zoom in and shrink each finger, her wrists, her arms. I bring in her waistline a few pixels at a time. I'm a child abuser, I'm a flesh-eating virus.

I'm a cartoonist. This is a joke.

It's quarter past five. I've been editing for three hours and I'm sixty-four seconds into the film. My work is all seconds and pixels and millimeters. My work is the size of a lifetime. I wonder if life seemed so long before I started looking at it one frame at a time. I'll be up here forever, fixing Mrs. Tyburn's memory. I'll stay up here forever until my parents come and climb the stairs, burst in and gather me up. Mrs. Tyburn will try to stop them. "She isn't finished. I still have bad memories up there. You can't have her until she's finished." But my mother will be awesome. "Back off, Madame Bovary!" she'll shout, and then probably flick out a switchblade or something embarrassing like that. And we'll go.

We'll live in one of those places you have to get to by train. I'll go back to school and learn French in no time. Or German or whatever. And we won't talk about anything in the past. We won't be able to. We'll live in a place where nothing has a memory, and I'll have a chance to catch up with the world.

I paste the frames I've been editing back into the parent file and play it at speed. There are a couple of hiccups. Pause, step back, tweak. I consider letting a couple of small errors slide but I never do. Someone *will* see this film after all. Just once. Mrs. Tyburn will watch all of these, one time, to replace her memory of the day with the spotless memory of a film of the day, and she's paying me to make the memory perfect.

Body-image garbage out of the way, it's time to rename the boat. The part I was really looking forward to. What I have in mind is like when Michelangelo painted one of his critics getting his tiny penis bitten off on the Sistine Chapel ceiling, or like the guy who did the artwork for the home video cover of *The Little Mermaid* and made one of the spires of Triton's castle in the shape of a huge cock. I go through frame after frame of footage putting the new name on the old boat—*Lolly*, my grandmother's nickname, the only name I ever called her. Everyone else called her Violet. As a joke, it's totally private, entirely my own. Kind of a prank, kind of an ode.

The repetition is making my mind wander. *Jenny*'s dead, long live *Lolly*. Out with *Jenny*, in with *Lolly*. *Jenny* off, *Lolly* on. When the boat turns away and appears to the camera at a coy angle, the letters need to shift too, Lolly on a red carpet looking at the cameras over her shoulder as her fans swoon and scream at their TV screens. She was never Grandma to me, or Granny or Nanna—always Lolly. Maybe I tried to say Violet when I was little and couldn't manage. I'll have to ask my mother, when I see her next, when she comes for me.

It's been almost four months since Lolly died. What started as soreness sprinted ahead with a power that didn't belong to human tissue. It was just an odd pain at first, a sore left breast. And then it turned red and sprouted streaking tendrils that reached out to her armpits, and her throat swelled up. But just as suddenly it went away and life went on. She worked in the garden, grinning and cooing at the furriness of bees in the lilacs or the discovery of an arrowhead in a turn of the soil. But it came back the next week. I was on the couch staring into a book one night when I heard her go, *hmmm*. The sound when just one question sounds like a million, a monster with too many identical heads. The next morning she went to the Oceanic for Gretchen to have a look. They said they needed to keep her there overnight for tests, whatever tests they could manage with the equipment they had on hand. And she died the next day, Sunday. Violet.

Lolly, Lolly, Lolly in every frame, on and on. My eyes are sore but I'm working faster now. It is starting to seem important—something like pride is welling up. It looks good, as if it had been that way all along.

"Oh, would you look at that."

I jump as if guilty. I hadn't heard Mrs. Tyburn come in, too absorbed in the playback, checking the smoothness of the text between frames.

"Marvelous, dear girl. Very well done. If I hadn't been there

I would have sworn that nothing had been done to this footage whatsoever."

I have to work hard to smile back at her. It's like that last push-up that makes you strain and grimace and grunt.

"Just one thing, my darling. I have to say, I'm not wild about *Lolly*. It makes one think about . . . licking." She makes a face. I hear my molars grind. I could kill you. I could rip out your throat with my teeth. "Could you change it to Priss? You don't mind, do you?" My smile grows wider and all of my features start to fall sideways off the edges of my face.

But she can't just leave. She has to go on: "You really work magic, you know. It's astounding. Magic."

She's paying me by the hour, so I really shouldn't care. It's her money. The waste is hers. My time is worth five dollars an hour. Eight cents a minute. It's pretty much a long-distance call. Dish out your money, you ignorant old bag. Sit there and toss dimes at me all day since you're too helpless to do anything else. Get someone to tug a smile onto your face and pin it in place today and I'll take care of all the days that you neglected. I'll do all the work that you didn't do.

When she finally does walk out, her bleached platinum head smug with her nice new history, I decide to claw back some time to look for my folks. I take out my list of places we've lived in and pick up where I left off. As the little fat yellow stick figure, grabbed by the scruff and dropped into Street View, I navigate systematically, inching my way around city blocks, checking out the blurry people, frozen in their errands. Everyone looks familiar, like no one in particular. I trawl the streets unseen for miles, scanning, chasing every promising body but always finding strangers' frames, alien limbs, the postures of other people's families under the pixilated faces. There's an ugly new apartment block on the lot where we picked dandelions that time; people are shuffling out of the food bank at the back of the church near our old house. When I finish one city, I slide the cursor to whatever city's next on the list and start again. It made me feel better at first; now it's starting to make me feel sick.

I can picture the maps of a dozen cities that all hang together now. Over the Brooklyn Bridge to emerge in South Boston. Down the Hollywood Hills to land in Boulder Valley. The straight lines are all illusions, the average of a collective point of view. Are the roads in Rome still straight? Would the strangers be too strange? Will I be too strange for the strangers that I meet out there when I have to go back to the Bad Place?

Do you know the story of the top and the ball? It was one of the short ones in the tattered book of bedtime stories that my dad had somehow smuggled from his own childhood. After "The Ugly Duckling" and before "The Little Match Girl." It was strange and never my favorite, about two toys who are in love until the ball gets lost and ends up warped by weather and neglect. How long will it be until me or my folks have weathered into a shape where we can't even recognize each other anymore? Or until we've changed so much we can't love each other again, like jigsaw puzzle pieces that have gotten wet and distorted and can't fit together, like they should, and the picture will never be right? I wonder if what I've lost is the possibility of fitting anywhere. An extraneous piece, the wrong blue for the sky or the sea, the wrong green for the leaves or the grass or the café awnings or the leather of the little boy's lederhosen.

My parents lost all the photos from my childhood in some move or other. I don't have the straw to spin into gold, the way I do it up here in Mrs. Tyburn's attic. My magic will work on her but not on me. I'll have to start from scratch, on my own, the old-fashioned way. Except they'll come back for me tomorrow. I know they will.

CHAPTER FOUR

Putting your phone on silent is supposed to be subtle, but that only works if you have it in your pocket or your bag or something. My phone is on the table, where it has a kind of seizure, knocking its back against the surface over and over, making so much noise you wish you'd just left it on. I'm too clumsy and fumble with it, and by the time I press the green button I've missed his call again. Jason's usual First Friday call. He can leave a message.

In the dorky story I play out in my head, Jason's my boyfriend. When he's not around and only exists in my mind, we have this perfect relationship. He surprises me with gifts, brings me flowers. No one has ever given me flowers before, and I hate how much pleasure the idea brings me. We stay up all night talking, and then go out on my lawn and watch the sun come up. I say that I need to go to bed, that I have to work the next day, but he won't let me go. "Just another minute. Five more minutes. Ten more," and he holds me tighter. He takes me to a family event on the mainland (on the boat I'm cool, relaxed, but he keeps me close, just in case), something middle-weight like a Memorial Day cookout. Nothing too serious like Christmas or anything. I'm nervous but he says everyone will love me, and they do. I find things to talk about with the grown-ups, and the kids all claim me as their favorite after I teach them how to walk on their hands. (In my imagination, I know how to walk on my hands.) But his mother loves me best of all. She always wanted a girl, and she thinks I'm "just darling." No, that sucks. It's more like: I bust out some super-witty one-liner and she says, "That's my girl," but quietly, mostly just for me to hear, and then tosses me a wink, a subtle wink—or is winking just too heinous?

His mom is pretty in the pictures on her Facebook page. But then again, she always untags herself from the ones where she looks kinda iffy. I probably won't ever meet her in real life, which is fine by me, actually. I'd probably like his imaginary mother better, and when I say the wrong thing in front of the imaginary mother I can just shake the scene like a huge Etch A Sketch and start over. ⌘+z. I have as many tries as I need to make it perfect.

My phone flashes again, alerting me to a voicemail.

"You have one new message," the robot voice tells me, adding gravely, "The next message is three minutes long." My voicemail only records for three minutes, so when I hear that it means that either someone has called me accidentally and recorded the noise in their bag or their back pocket, or that it's the first Friday of the month and my imaginary boyfriend's stoned and rambling.

"Hey, it's me. Just calling 'cause I'm on the island and wondered if you want to meet up. But I guess you're not there. Maybe you're at work or something. So, I don't know if you're busy or whatever . . ."

I prop the phone between my shoulder and my ear, half listening while I get back to work re-renaming the dickhead boat, waiting for an important detail to emerge from Jason's monologue. I think he thinks that voicemail is like old-fashioned answering machines, the kind that would click on and play aloud in the room, giving the other person time to race to the landline and pick up. It's a cell phone. Where does he think I'm not?

I text back a reply answering the questions I picked out from his white noise of "ums" and "ahs." "Finish work at 6. Pick me up at Mrs. T's. Happy to help finish up your rounds. Will be fun."

———

Quitting time. I've done a lot today; I'm getting faster. I could finish this in my lifetime, maybe even in hers. I have a notebook where I jot down what I've done that day and where I've stopped. It's a pain in the ass if I lose my place, and the log also helps Mrs. Tyburn feel like she's keeping an eye on what I'm doing, like otherwise I might sit up here jerking off all day. I take the external hard drive and make sure everything's backed up. I shut down, spray the keyboard, wipe the screen, push in my chair, and take my teacup with me. It's like no one's been here.

I find Mrs. Tyburn in the living room. There's some kind of jazzy piano music on. It must be old. Sounds like a CD of a really scratchy recording. She's drinking a martini, which is probably one of the top five sexiest things people can do. I make a mental note to develop a taste for them.

"Finished for the day, my dear?" She looks at her watch and smiles at me. I wish it was easier to read her face. The clock on the mantelpiece says it's just after six.

"Yeah, I got to a good stopping point. I've marked the logbook and—"

Just then the doorbell rings.

"Gentleman caller?"

I don't really know what to say, so I end up spitting out something stupid like, "Kinda . . . Jason." But she knew that. Who else would it be?

"First Friday already? Oh, how one's mind goes all to dots."

I laugh with her even though I'm not sure I get the joke. Maybe I'm supposed to disagree, tell her she's sharp as hell, that she's got the mind of a teenage Einstein and a fantastic rack to boot, but I'm tired and I don't want to play games with Geriatric Barbie. I just want to get out of here. But she has to keep talking.

"Funny that you should be the one with a regular visitor."

It's so awkward I can hardly breathe. "He's here for Giddy and for the others, not really to see me. You know that. I just kind of help . . ."

"Nonsense. Nothing wrong with taking on a beau at your age. So these are your *going out* clothes?"

"I guess . . . I didn't really bring much with me when I came over, so sometimes I have to borrow my grandmother's clothes."

"Violet always did strike a bit of style, God bless her soul. I'd give you some of my old things but I'm just so awfully petite."

The doorbell rings again.

"Go on, now. Don't leave your suitor at the threshold. The way you linger anyone would think you're simply loath to abandon me."

I walk over and kiss the air next to each of her cheeks. "See you on Monday, Mrs. Tyburn."

She reaches into the drawer of the end table next to her, takes out an envelope with my week's wages, and hands it to me. "Until Monday, my darling."

I open the door and Jason looks up and blows out a mouthful of cigarette smoke, and we stand there for a minute, looking at each other.

His eyes are Thanksgiving-turkey brown and he has a smile out of a catalog. His whole look would be too pretty, too all-American white boy, if it wasn't for the little imperfections, the scar over his right eye, the cigarette always hanging from his lips or pressed between his yellowed fingers, the little rips of skin by his fingernails. His disheveled short brown hair makes him look like a newborn kitten. And even though he's always got sour nicotine breath, his kisses, even a little peck hello, always get to me.

"You're back," I say when we pull apart from our hello kiss.

"I'm back." He smiles again and does a half laugh before he turns and we start off together down the path toward the center of the island.

"How's Giddy?" I ask him, even though I saw his grandmother myself in Rose's shop yesterday. She'll be different for him than she is for me, anyway. Giddy smiles, says hello, tolerates me. As we make our way over to Suzie and Johnny at the Psychedelicatessen, he tells me about their day together, getting stoned and planting winter veggies in Giddy's garden plot, digging new beer traps for slugs. She made cucumber soup for lunch, and they talked about the latest book for their two-person book club. Giddy called him out for not finishing it before she confessed to dropping it herself a chapter after he had. He's animated, like the day's been an adventure, like he would love her even if he didn't have to, like he'd come to see his grandmother even if he wasn't obliged. I manage to contain the jealousy before it gets to be too much.

He laces his fingers between mine and squeezes. "How've *you* been?"

"Yeah, good." I wish I had something to tell him, but nothing's changed. I take my hand away and put it across my eyebrows to keep the sun out of my eyes. "I've been changing the name of Mrs. Tyburn's husband's boat."

It doesn't sound as difficult and complicated when I say it like that.

"In a home movie, frame by frame," I add. Walking wakes me up a bit after the day cooped up in the edit suite. And the island is beautiful. It seems made for summer. The spaces between the houses are green with wispy grasses and wildflowers, or lumpy with funny stacks of rocks and moss. It's not uptight like a suburb with buzz-cut lawns and prissy flower beds. The island is like someone who's really pretty and knows she looks better without makeup. The sea is silver and reflect-y like a crumpled piece of foil.

Most of the Swans ignore younger visitors, but everyone nods to Jason when they pass us, even though he's only twenty-two. Jason's essential here. When First Friday rolls around, and the handful of younger relatives and Wrinkly friends who can't or won't leave the mainland come over, Jason visits his grandmother, Giddy. He comes every month, our most regular guest. They talk and eat, take walks. He fixes things around her house or helps in her garden plot, reminds her of her Facebook password so they can look at the latest photos his mother has posted.

And then he gets to work.

In front of the swirly rainbow walls of the Psychedeli, Johnny is washing out a massive stockpot with the hose while Suzie sits in the grass in her big red cat's-eye glasses reading on her Kindle, skirt hitched up to get some sun on her pale, freckled legs.

When Johnny sees us, he lifts his big, leather-vested torso and waves us over, shouting, "Jason! What's up, dude?" He drops the hose and splashes Suzie.

She waves her e-reader at him. "Old man, you wreck this hundred-dollar rock and I'll have your hide with my eggs tomorrow!" She reaches for Jason's arm and he hitches her up and gets pulled right into a hug. "Ain't you here right on time! Come on in, you two."

Johnny turns off the water and follows us in with the clean pot, which he carries as if it weighs nothing.

Inside, blue walls painted with a cloudscape that mimics the sky on a clear summer day gives the Psychedeli a great feeling of spaciousness, which it needs against the hodgepodge of home-made and salvaged furniture and pillows and beanbags that make up the dining room. Hardly anyone uses the beanbags because it's hard to get up once you're in one, even for me, and they always talk about getting rid of them but never do. They've hung some flags over the counter at the back, all with acronyms like POW-MIA and AFL-CIO, and ones with the Led Zeppelin zeppelin and the Rolling Stones lips. It smells like a health food store in a small town. The almost creamy scent from boiling fresh bagels in the morning blankets the room, sweetened with the lingering haze of the sage they burn and the grass they grow and the oomph of coffee brewing strong in their big urn. Coffee costs a nickel here, just like newspapers.

Having stowed the pot in the kitchen, Johnny comes back with a coffee each for Jason and me, and we settle into the purple-cushioned booth at the back, discreet, even though there aren't many customers—just one table where Helen and Nancy are having tea while Marie reads Joanna's tarot cards—because Suzie hasn't rung the food bell yet. It's a ritual that Mrs. Tyburn hates (you can hear it almost everywhere on the island, except the really far-out places like Lolly's house), but as usual, Mrs. Tyburn's dainty sensibilities are nothing against the hippie consensus.

"Man, you get skinnier every time I see you. They don't have food in the Bad Place no more?" Johnny says gruffly as he turns back toward the kitchen.

"I see your wife's still keeping you in the clean-plate club." Jason gives him a little punch in his biker gut and they kind of hug and do a sloppy wannabe-hip handshake-low-five thing.

Suzie follows with sugar, milk, and a couple of spoons. "You better watch that mouth when you're talking to my old man. You're not too big for me to put you over my knee."

"No, but *he* is," says Jason, pointing a thumb at Johnny.

"Don't bet on it," Johnny corrects him, back at the table now with a parcel the size of a large shoebox, like one you'd put a pair of boots in. He slides it across the table to Jason and gives Suzie a squeeze and a big *mwah* kind of kiss. Jason takes a smaller package and pushes it across to Johnny.

The shoebox Johnny gives to Jason is the island's only export, Swan Silver, what they're cooking upstairs at the Psychedelica-tessen, a hybrid of AK-47 and White Widow. Hydroponic, organic, anti-inflammatory, and, apparently, better than Sudoku for the early signs of Alzheimer's. I did a spit-take when they first told me it fetches twenty dollars a gram. But then they let me try it.

They keep the growing discreet, a concession to the Swans who feel antsy about the whole thing. Nobody really expects a bunch of sweet old-timers to get raided, but the world they've made for themselves is too precious to expose to the whims of cops. So they keep the operation small. Only a few plants, but it's enough to make sure that even when a market blip drains someone's pension, or a member of someone's family needs to get buried back in the Bad Place, everyone has what they need. Jason collects the stock, sells it on the mainland, and brings back the proceeds. This cash fills up Swan Bank every month, and the money there is free. No questions asked. That is, if you're old enough.

Johnny draws a half-cup gulp of his coffee and drawls, "Right, you bad little tadpole. What've you got for us this fine summer's day?"

Jason pulls a good-size Tupperware container out of his backpack. "I'm sure we'll be able to find something you can handle, Grandpa."

"Can I box his ears now?" Suzie asks me.

Until she says that I thought everyone had forgotten that I was there. And since when do I make decisions about Jason's ears? Maybe it's because we've been doing this for a while, and the past few times they've seen Jason I've always been with him. The moment starts to feel like a totally weird double date, but I don't *not* like it.

"Be my guest—saves me having to do it." When you have no idea what to say, and out of nowhere comes a little one-liner that makes everyone laugh, God should congratulate you. Not that it was even funny, really, but Suzie Q laughs her big-smile laugh and Johnny nudges Jason. It's been ages since I've felt this relaxed.

"'Atta girl."

But Johnny really just wants Jason to open up the box and get down to business. "Did you get any more of those nice Ecuadorian shrooms in?"

"Didn't manage it, but I've got some High Hawaiians I think you'll like even better." He pushes some baggies and brown plastic bottles aside and pulls out a brown paper bag. Johnny opens it quickly with his big, calloused fingers and takes a whiff. His eyebrows do a little dance in time with his laugh.

"Boy, I think you're onto something with that!"

Jason takes them through the whole selection—three strains of magic mushrooms, a vial of super-clean liquid LSD, smiley-faced ecstasy tablets, and little jewelry bags of MDMA crystals, tight origami wraps of coke, bottles of Adderall and Dexedrine, Viagra and Cialis he sells individually or buy-ten-get-one-free. They end up with an ounce of the High Hawaiians, half a dozen E pills, and twelve doses of LSD, which they drop onto blotter paper to keep in the freezer for a rainy day.

Suzie starts laughing as she tries to get the next sentence out. "Last time we got a stash of the Hawaiians, remember that night, Johnny? We got so twisted we were convinced Helen got lost. Went over and rang the bell, popped into her and Nancy's place and she wasn't there. Went into the Relic and Rose's and wasn't there neither. Looking everywhere, brains all tangled in a tizzy. Spent an hour wandering the north side looking for her before we realized she was helping us look! Remember that, Helen tapping me and sayin', 'Suzie, who we lookin' fer again?'"

Johnny and Suzie wet themselves laughing (sorry, I shouldn't say that; I just meant it like a figure of speech). While they're busting their guts about the light side of memory loss, I remember I have something I meant to return.

"Hey, Johnny." It's hard to get a word in, they're still laughing so hard. I take the cassettes Johnny lent me out of my bag—six bootleg tapes in dirty plastic cases held together by a rubber band.

"What'd ya think of them?"

"Yeah, really good." They're bootlegs of old Grateful Dead shows. "I recognized some of the songs from stuff my parents used to play. But the sound quality . . . What, were you recording a show in a sandstorm?"

I know that wasn't exactly hilarious but I'm still surprised when no one laughs. I mean, they're not exactly hard to please. "I only listened to them once 'cause it's only going to get worse the more they get played."

Johnny gives a big *duh* eye roll and purses unimpressed lips through his facial hair.

I'm confused. "So," I go on, a little hesitant. "I digitized them for you. Check your email—you can store the tapes and play the MP3s now."

Everything I say seems like I'm announcing another Bush presidency.

Johnny picks up the bundle of tapes and kind of points at me with them. "Every time I think you're getting to be a down lady, you miss the point completely."

Everyone's silence pools around me as Johnny's meaning starts to sink in. That things are *supposed* to wear out, that it's not a problem we have to solve, or a process that needs to be stopped in its tracks like something out of a commercial for wrinkle cream that makes looking like an old lady sound like the worst thing an old lady could ever do. Wearing out doesn't mean something's broken. It means it's doing what it's supposed to be doing.

And that's how everything is here. Not that everyone feels like you have to *grow old gracefully* or whatever. Just that everyone's allowed to do it their own way, but the fact is that they're getting old—same as me, really. Rose always says that we're all the same age because we're all the oldest we've ever been. I think that's her way of helping me not feel left out.

"Well." Suzie breaks the silence, hoisting herself up by the back of the seat. "Me and this mean ol' grizzly best get tonight's grub on the fire. Jason, you get home safe now, ya hear? Pack the smelly shit up tight. Don't want no trouble with the Coast Guard."

"I will, Suzie. Thanks."

"And you, missy, you give that man o' yers something to *eat*."

"Oh, *she will* . . ." Johnny does his stupid eyebrow dance and laughs at his own super-awesome joke.

Gross.

"*Ignore* him. Y'all mind how you go. Don't do nothing what can't be fixed with glue or a big ol' smooch."

They walk us out, stand on the porch, and wave goodbye.

Next stop is the Oceanic. Frances has an easel set up on the porch, painting the sunset. Which is appropriate because if you think about it, really good sunsets always look like really bad paintings of sunsets.

I look out at the view as well. I think my mother's hand is moving across the sea, smoothing it like a sheet, like my hair or my forehead. She's thinking about me. Right now. I can feel her thinking about me.

The medical setup here is pretty spontaneous, and Jason's part of it. It's not chaotic; the doctors and nurses just do what they think they need to do when situations arise. The equipment is sparse, used, ordered off the internet or obtained through connections in the last places they worked before Swan. Most of the pharmaceuticals come from the internet, ordered in bulk and sent to a shared post-office box in Portsmouth. And Jason's the only non-Swan with a key.

Gretchen and Jason hug and she starts talking to him right away, about one of the Swans who's just come back from Boston and his final round of chemo. She doesn't seem to have seen me. I know she has a thing for Jason. Whether they ever did anything, before I came or whatever, I never asked, and he never mentioned. Neither did Rose, and if anyone would have known, she would. Anyway, it's none of my business. It's not like he's exactly my boyfriend. He's more like a period, something that happens to my vagina once a month. No, that's mean. I'm just trying to say I don't feel possessive about him, that's all. He's a friend, an imaginary boyfriend at best. My life is way too fucked up for anything serious anyway, and he never, like, pops out to Swan for a visit. Obviously. But maybe this time he could stay. Just sleep over, I mean. If he feels like it. No big deal.

"Mind the cat, dear," Gretchen says to me out of nowhere. While I'm still trying to process what she said, I actually do trip over the cat and only just catch myself before my chin hits the floor. Gretchen and Jason help me up—it feels like being confused is making my body heavier, and it's weird when something simple like *getting up* becomes a three-person job. Sexy, *real* sexy. Whenever Jason's around I become the clumsiest person in town, which is saying something.

It's Germaine, the obnoxious little monster Joanna brought back from the Bad Place last month along with the new defibrillator machine. It looks like a toy tiger, almost cartoonishly orange with black stripes, and it turns to growl and hiss at me through its squashed face with one wet fang poking down out of one side of its mouth. They say that contact with an animal reduces blood pressure; I hope it works for the Wrinklies better than it has for me.

Hit the nail on the head with the name; that cat's a Germaine if I ever saw one. Luckily, before I asked why they didn't get a kitten instead of Snaggle Tooth here, I realized exactly why. *We don't worship youth here, cuteness is* not *a virtue, inexperience isn't an excuse, naivete is tedious.* I almost tell the Rose-voice in my head, Yeah, yeah, I get it. Not a kitten. A cat.

"You okay?" Jason asks.

"Yeah. Just embarrassed." I try to whisper so it can be between us, but it doesn't work and Gretchen kind of giggle-coughs. At the doorway to her office, she takes the package of pills and potions Jason brought over, places it on her desk, and locks the door behind her. She's really pretty.

We climb the stairs and go past the Duchess's room. Clack, bleep, suck, drop.

"How is she?" Jason asks.

I start to answer but Gretchen gets there first. I guess he was *actually* talking to her, anyway. I mean, why would he ask me when her doctor's standing right there?

"Nothing from her for ages, I'm afraid. She hasn't got long."

"I'm sorry." He sounds like he really means it. And I know he does. That's one of the things I love about Jason. He'd rather be silent than say some stupid bullshit he doesn't mean, or ask a question he doesn't care about the answer to just to make noise. Jason's not afraid to be quiet.

A couple of doors down from the Duchess is Ernie's room.

"Jason, my main man!" Ernie always calls him that.

"What's up, Ernie?" They do a complicated little dude handshake and Ernie pulls a newspaper off the table next to his window so Jason can put down his case and start the tour through this week's selection.

When I first met Jason, I suggested that it would make things easier if everyone just met at the Psychedeli to buy gear instead of making Jason do the whole circuit of Swan. But even all the way out here, the Wrinklies still think it makes sense to be discreet. And anyway, old people really like house calls.

Ernie takes some Swan Silver for his glaucoma and Jason throws in a couple of mushrooms just to be sweet. Joanna says a bong hit's the only thing that works for her bad back and her arthritic ankle. Louise just likes getting high and goes in for a range, from her cut of the island crop to the ethically murky South American blow.

Then she asks what everyone else has picked up so far. When Jason tells her that Johnny and Suzie bought some E, she adds two hits to her order and starts sending Suzie a text message as soon as she's said goodbye to us.

Gretchen shows us out and says goodbye in this really head-tilty way, which I'm not sure is flirtatious or condescending, or maybe I should check my head and stop being so goddamn paranoid.

Halfway down the steps, Jason gives the hand-holding a second attempt, sliding his palm against mine, lacing our fingers together, giving my hand a little squeeze. "Any luck?"

He means finding my parents.

"Tommy, the friend of theirs who said he'd ask around—I called him every day last week and yesterday he finally answered his fucking phone. Then it took me five minutes to explain who I was and what I was calling about. Then he was all, 'Oh, right. You're that kid. You wanted your parents to call you?' and I was like, 'Yeah,' and he's all, 'I don't have their number no more but I can ask around.' *Totally fucking forgot*."

Jason makes a *tsk* noise and rolls his eyes.

"But he gave me another of their friends' cell-phone numbers. Mia. She was nice enough. Said she saw them about six months ago, trying to get the deposit together for an apartment in Pittsburgh."

"Why Pittsburgh?"

"Got me."

Just then three blond Swans, Grace, Agata, and Ruth, pass by on their daily run. They're the types that go all out, sports bras and spandex shorts and proper running shoes that look like they were designed by NASA. They wave and say hi to Jason and me and leave us in their dust.

"Anyway, maybe if they're trying to settle down somewhere, they'll get in touch."

Jason stops and pulls me into a hug. He's trying to comfort me. But something about it just makes it all hurt so much worse, and I catch my face starting to sting and I can't let myself, I can't let myself get started now, because if I do I'll have another goddamn ocean gushing out of my face, and that's the last thing I need.

Sometimes when people hug you, it's really sweaty, or your bodies don't fit together very well and there's something weird about the bend of your arm or where your shoulder has to go. But Jason is perfect; I mean, he's not *perfect*. We are. We fit.

I pull away. "I'm feeling pretty optimistic, actually. I don't know—I just have a feeling they're going to call. Soon."

"How long are you gonna wait?"

"It's not like they'd just leave me and never come back. They'll call."

Jason doesn't believe me. Not in a mean way. He just doesn't pretend he knows that everything's going to be fine.

"I just can't leave until I know they're okay. If I split, they won't know how to get in touch with me and I won't have any way to contact them and then that's it."

"I'm sorry."

I don't want to talk about it anymore. "So, who's left?"

"Nick's got a half O coming from the island yield."

"My fan club. Great." I'd hate to see how uptight that guy would be without his ration of weed.

"At least it's on the way back to your place."

At least there's that . . .

Jason knows how Nick feels about me, so he doesn't press me to go in with him. I settle in a patch of tall grass and woody daisies in what's left of my backyard and wait for him. He joins me a few minutes later and takes a couple of beers out of his backpack, staring at the view with a skeptical look in his eyes. It's a look that says he can tell something's different but he can't put his finger on it. He opens the bottles with his lighter, hands one to me, and then lights the joint he's been keeping behind his ear.

"How are things in Rye?" I ask him.

"Bobby got locked up." Bobby is Jason's older brother.

"Shit. How long for?"

"Don't know yet. Some dick must have snitched, 'cause they busted into his house just after he got a shipment in. Two kilos, uncut."

"God. I'm really sorry."

"It'll be his first conviction, so it probably won't be for too long."

We sit and sip our beers in silence for a while. Jason finishes his and opens another. The sky is changing color, like caramel cooking, moving from a pale, clear day into a sweeter, richer twilight. I lean against Jason's chest and stare into the tall grass. The sound of the waves breathing mixes with the bugs and bees, the crickets and gulls. Jason finishes his second beer. I've forgotten about mine.

"Should we go in?" He sounds shy. For some reason I find that really—I don't know—exciting maybe. I lead the way around back and up the two steps to the kitchen door.

"That step's still broken."

"Yeah, I keep forgetting to have someone look at it."

People say weird things when they're about to have sex. But it's not like you can talk about what you're about to do. The fact that you're about to do pretty much the weirdest thing that people do can make *everything* seem really bizarre.

Jason starts kissing me as soon as we're through the kitchen door. I don't know whether to call the kisses hard or soft—maybe they're both, like a cock, like the way they make me ache and strain and gush in my underwear.

I go into my room first and he follows but doesn't close the door all the way, so I have to go back and push the door until it clicks. He looks at me as if to ask why, what's the point, since no one is here. And I pretend not to notice.

He takes his shirt off and then pulls my face to his with both hands. Right away I start to heat up. It's amazing and really uncomfortable at the same time, like what I want is going to overwhelm me, make me lose my grip, lose control. Part of me starts to wish he would just leave.

He puts his right hand under my shirt and cups my breast and kind of strokes my nipple with his thumb in this way that he does, with the perfect amount of pressure like some kind of nipple engineer. (Wait, what?) He starts moaning a little and I do too while we kiss, and it's nice, like we're singing to each other, some song only we can hear. Low and almost growly, like dinosaurs singing to each other. I don't know what that means but that's what it makes me think of. He's hard now, and so am I, I guess, if that's what you call it.

Then he steps toward the bed and I step backward, and we start taking each other's clothes off, unfastening belts and buttons, pulling down zippers, and tugging on belt loops. As we finally collapse on the bed, instead of fumbling with the hooks on my bra, he pulls it up over my head intact. It's uncomfortable and my boobs flop out in a super-*not*-glamorous way. It makes me wonder if he's got a girl on the mainland with much smaller tits than mine. Not that I care. It's not like I'm his girlfriend or anything. I have no right to be jealous, and I'm totally not.

I scoot further onto the bed and we both pull down our underwear. Looking into his eyes is really just a way not to have to look at his hard-on, this weird, awkward thing.

Jason's kissing my breasts and I take the opportunity to reach into the bedside drawer and pull out a condom. I put it on him quickly and then I lean back for the moment when he . . . *enters* me. I read it put like that in a collection of erotic short stories a friend and I snuck down from her parents' bookshelf when we were kids and now I can't get it out of my head. Strange. Accurate, but too precise. Every time I have sex with some guy there's always that moment when he *enters* me, like I'm a goddamn eighth-grade essay contest.

I'm pretty worked up and he slips in easily, back and forth, building up friction, burning more and more. He sighs, like he's never been more comfortable in his whole life. It's this deep "h" noise and he makes a pretty stupid face with it. I realize I must be making stupid faces too; I try to soften my grimace into some kind of smile. I pull my head back, press my crown into the pillow. I love this. I love it. I match his "huhs" with "ahs." When he goes deeper my voice gets higher, in volume and in pitch. Sometimes because I think I should, but sometimes it just comes out.

He starts going faster and I brace my hips against the force. He seems to like it and lets his head down, kissing me, and we sing into each other's mouth again, weird singing, fucking mammal dinosaurs. I try to bring my mind back. I'm here, fucking my imaginary boyfriend, and it's amazing. He's got a good cock. Not too big, but better than that one time when I went out with a jock. The first time we fooled around I found out why he'd chosen pole-vaulting instead of running track or doing the high jump or whatever. We were naked and, you know, just fooling around, and then I noticed this weird look on his face. It took me ages before I realized that he was fucking me. I mean, I couldn't even *tell*. Just by the look on his face. But, like, he didn't ask or anything, and I was so shocked that I didn't know what to do. And just when I got it together in my head enough to tell him to stop—and keep in mind this is taking place over the course of seconds, like, three or four *seconds*—he pulled out and came on my stomach. I avoided him for a few days (mostly I just didn't go to school) and then broke it off. We were too different. He was a jock, all set with a college scholarship and everything, and I was just the weird new girl who read books all the time and never talked to anyone. He shrugged it off but I could tell he was hurt. I had an abortion six weeks later. Hitting him up for his half of the money was just too much hassle. The first time of many I've blown all my savings on a pointless mistake.

Spiky, mean thoughts try to pry their way in, but I shoo them away. I say *it wasn't my fault, it wasn't my fault, it wasn't my fault, it wasn't my fault*.

This is real and now is real, and I'm here and it's so hot our bodies stick and graft and it hurts to touch and hurts to pull apart.

Oh, God. I'm dying and I'm alone. I'm dying and no one cares because we're all dying, we're all flying through space at the same rate.

"Faster . . ."

and sometimes it's too mundane, to die a little every single day and sometimes you can feel it, you can feel how fast we're flying through space and

"It's amazing."

He kisses me to thank me for the compliment. When he takes his mouth away again I want to say I'm dying but maybe that's not exactly what he wants to hear.

It's all mixed in my head, everything's mixed up. It's like, I didn't want you anyway, just leave me the fuck alone but if you stop I'll fucking kill you. Do you hear me? Fucking. Kill. You. But of course he doesn't hear me because this is all just a blur of nonsense thoughts and sensations that's sometimes like a kaleidoscope, all colors and brightness, and sometimes that muddled nothing color that happens when you're a kid and you mix all the Play-Doh together and your mom shouts that you've ruined it now but how were you supposed to know—

"Oh God, keep doing that."

"What?"

"That."

"That?"

"Oh God."

Oh shit, I can't remember his name. I was just about to yell it out. It's—sometimes it's, it's—sometimes it's nice to be encouraging when they're doing something good or even when, when, even when it's not going so well, it's nice to say something because you've got to make noise, I mean, when you're making noise already and it's nice—

"Oh, Jason."

Aha! Jason, of course—it's good, to encourage them, so they know how it's going and saying their name makes it, makes it, makes it, like, oh, personal. It's nice, it's a nice thing to do. Women and children first, women and children first. We're inside each other and he's got me surrounded and suddenly I feel perfect and perfect and perfectly sure that I'm going to die very soon, maybe even now, maybe even in the moment that was now and just passed and I'm gushing my life out like a fat, bleeding bee.

There's a man in my bed. Not my man, really. And in a way it's not even my bed. But they're both mine now. The springs press into my right side and his hand rests on my left side.

"Your hair's all messed up."

"So what."

We stare into each other's eyes until we can't stand it anymore. The pressure builds until kissing more is the only way to release it. Pressing our lips together, biting his earlobe, kissing my collarbone, pressing his nose into my sternum, rolling him over, squeezing each other hard, resting my ear on his chest.

"Your heart's beating really fast."

"So's yours. I can feel it in my stomach."

This is what we do, my imaginary boyfriend and his little castaway.

The light at the window's turning red.

I trace my finger over the curve of his shoulder and lean up and bite it. He half squeals and laughs, rolls me over, pins my arms down, and starts kissing me. Harder and harder until he reaches down and I hear the foil of another condom ripping and we're at it again.

After our second go we sit up and share a joint. We must look like a married couple. I nestle my shoulder into his armpit and lean against him.

"What time's Ted taking you back over to Appledore?"

I don't know why I ask that. He'll go when he always goes.

"Eight. Need to get moving soon."

"You can stay here, if you want. I'll cook. Are you hungry?" Boys are always hungry.

"Um, yeah, but I gotta get back tonight. It's busy on the weekend. All the Wrinklies counting on me to shift their gear, ya know?"

Just stay. They can miss you in the Bad Place for one night. Stay here, make some phone calls if you need to, rearrange your plans while I make us dinner. And then we can go for a walk on the north side of the island, out along the rocks. We can watch the sun set and maybe watch a movie on TV. Just stay tonight.

He pulls on his underwear, plain black boxers, not new, not worn out either. "I'm sorry. Maybe next time."

"Yeah, cool. No worries."

"Do you want any weed?"

I nod and reach for my bag to take out some money but he refuses. Instead he drops an eighth on the bedside table and leans over, kissing me again, giving this whole *it's so hard to leave you* routine, which he keeps going with until I push him away.

"Come on, you don't want to miss Ted. He's waiting."

He looks over at my alarm clock—"Shit"—and picks up the pace with getting dressed. "I'm sorry, I really wish I could stay."

It's weird being naked while he's dressed. I don't like it at all and I wish he'd just leave already if he has to.

"I'll call you," he says as he leaves without looking back at me.

My bed is comfortable. This bed, the guest bed. I listen to his footsteps down the stairs, across the living room, through the kitchen; the door closes really gently behind him. I move into the middle of the bed, splay my arms and legs out, relieved to be alone again, no talking, no repeating myself. No one to see the silly faces I make. I look up at the shapes made by bumps and depressions in the ceiling. An owl. An eel. A sea monster . . .

CHAPTER FIVE

Sometimes my parents were amazing. Like when Mom was still singing and she auditioned for a band that had just gotten signed and we went to California. We had a cool car that never broke down, an electric-blue Mustang convertible my parents loved. We drove fast with the top down. At least, I always remember us going fast.

California was strange as well, though. I was little (five? six?), and *California* felt like a magic word. So I didn't understand why California wasn't clean, why I didn't turn blond and golden there, why I still felt small for my height, and lonely. Why there was always this patina of dirt clinging to the hair on the palm trees, why the scars from mosquito bites still lingered big and black and ashy on my legs. Soon I developed a knack for looking at things without thinking about them. It helped. I just noticed the strangeness, the distance between me and everything else. The cars as they stopped at the traffic light outside my window, the letters on signs sitting bulky against their backgrounds, all these people who didn't seem to see me.

It did feel magical when we drove to their friends' houses in

Laurel Canyon. Out of the strip-mall lanes of the city, beyond the concrete and beige of the freeway, the drive turned dense green with lots of different leaves, occasional bald spots of desert with tufts of bushes threatening to become tumbleweeds. I could lose myself in the landscape going by, so the scars on my legs didn't matter so much. Once I was bored at one of their parties. There were two kids I could have played with, but they were lying on their stomachs at the edge of the pool, picking up fallen leaves from the patio and placing them on the surface of the water while they told each other secrets that seemed very important. I didn't like that game. I kept my distance and watched for a while, then walked into the house and found my parents in the kitchen with a handful of grown-ups, all talking at once, their jewelry rattling with their laughter. There was a pile of white rainbow glitter on the counter. I went to stick my finger in it, but as soon as I touched it the tall blonde who lived there pulled me away and slapped the dust off my fingers. She hauled me over to the sink, knocking my ribs against the edge, and rubbed her hands against mine under icy-cold water. "No! That is *not* for you!" Drying my hands on a limp little towel, she was only wearing a bikini and didn't seem to notice that one of her breasts had come out. I couldn't keep from staring at it. She knelt down to look me in the face. "There now—I wonder what the other kids are up to. Why don't you all get into your suits and play Marco Polo in the pool? How's that sound?" I nodded and went back outside, but instead I found a corner at the side of the pool house where I could be alone to cry.

And another night in Laurel Canyon—or maybe it was that same night, or maybe it wasn't in Laurel Canyon at all—my mother was up on an outdoor stage with the band behind her, wearing this incredible green dress with green and gold beads that looked like it had belonged to some kind of princess at the beginning of the twentieth century but got blown apart and stepped on and fucked with until its ripped-up remnants flattered my mother's licorice arms and serious thighs perfectly. Her sphere of hair was tinged with gold; her legs and arms and dress were a monster as the music started. Watching it was like picking up something you didn't realize was hot. The drums and bass started rolling, the guitar whined into time with the rhythm section; then she screamed and everything went electric. Her voice could slide from a siren to a growl like her body was an instrument from hell or the future. I thought the microphone would break in half and let out sparks every time she slammed her rings and claws into it. The noise made my eardrums and back teeth sting, and I knew I was seeing something important. I thought, this is us. This is what our lives are now.

But the best thing about it was my dad's face watching her. I wanted in on it, somehow. Part of me wanted to ask to be picked up; I just wanted a bit of what was in his eyes. I held out as long as I could before I raised my arms up to him, feeling like a bit of a baby. He scooped me up and held me and looked at me, really took a moment and looked at me, and then he turned his face back to the stage and it felt like we were looking at her together.

Later that night—or was it? How can I be sure? In the reel of my memory it's the same night, static from the show still tingling the surface of our little life. Still in California, anyway, and she's wearing the amazing green dress. My parents have left their bedroom door ajar and I'm watching them through the crack. He's painting her toenails black, blowing on her toes. They're talking about people I don't know. He stretches his body up along her legs and kisses her fingers. She kneels in front of him on the bed, and he comes up to his knees too, and she piles all her jewelry onto him from the bedside table, kisses her lipstick onto his mouth. She reaches over again to get her camera and takes a picture. I remember the electric snap of the flash.

Then she says she's going to paint his toes. He jumps up, which startles me and makes me jump too, and I brace myself for what I know will come next. Daddy, dripping with Mommy's beads and rhinestones, bounds upright onto the bedroom floor while she gets to her feet, bounces a couple of times on the bed, and launches herself, all those sparkly green arms, at the spot where he's standing. I hear her falling against him. Mom into Dad, Dad into door, door into my face, front tooth onto the floor. They're laughing in this sparkling pile—they haven't even noticed me—and for what feels like forever I don't know how to get them to see the blood on my hands and running down my nightgown.

If I had been at school then, and the teacher had asked me to draw a picture of my family, it would have been just like that: green glitter parents in a giggling pile, and me on the other side of the door frame, brown and pink with a terrible spill of red that keeps spreading, and plain, blank, paper white all around where the edges of my memory can't come up with any detail.

And then I'm in our kitchen. I know the walls in that kitchen were green with pink edges, but in my memory of that night the walls are paper white and my daddy is smiling at me and making cartoon voices so I smile back. He says I look cool with my missing front tooth. Tough. But I can't smile for very long and when it hurts too much I put my face into his neck and he closes around me like the whole entire world.

Then *I'm* wearing the green dress, in love with its weight, and my parents are tangled in a heap on the floor. And the air is flowery and spicy like nectar and sap. Did we walk through a forest that smelled like this? Was it Seattle, not LA? They're on the rug, breathing like dragons and shining their eyes at me while I sing Mommy's song to them in Mommy's dress, standing on a chest of drawers by an open window with the lights sitting gently on the city like my dad in all my mother's jewelry and my mother reclining long in a black silk slip.

It's been a long time since I heard her sing.

The California sky turns light blue. I pour myself a bowl of cereal. I've always heard grown-ups talking about the sunrise like it's something magical, so I go to the window to watch, listening to my parents breathing in their sleep, trying not to get milk on the green dress and failing. The colors in the sky change. I thought I'd change too but I don't. Daddy's lips are still a little pink with Mom's lipstick.

———

The sea is supposed to be soothing. Maybe I can isolate the sound without seeing it in my mind's eye. I can pretend it's the sound of pebbles falling, like those annoying rain sticks that middle-class hippies always have in their houses. Or beaded curtains swaying. Finally I'm falling into sleep listening to the push and pull, the pound and splash, the stupid sea that's everywhere, the dumb wet thing that's got me surrounded, and oh God, I'm going to have to take a shower tomorrow, maybe I should just get it over with now, and anyway it'll be nice to be clean when they get here. I'll tidy the house, I'll cook.

Calm down. There's plenty of time to take care of everything. In this moment, everything's fine. They promised they'd be back. They have to come. They have to.

You fucking bastards, where are you?

Sea sounds, pull, push, lift-and-drop, blah, blah, blah. Big bully that doesn't know when to stop, slapping the cliff that holds up my house just because it's bigger and it can.

Fuck it, it's too early to sleep. Never mind.

I pull on a T-shirt and some underwear and go downstairs. I remember the newspaper I bought this morning, toss it from my bag onto the couch, and turn on the TV for background noise. It's much harder to take the news when you're in a room alone. Wednesday's paper, but it doesn't matter. I thought it would bother me, never being able to get the paper the day it comes out. The Swans buy newspapers like history books. They're not fussed that a few days have passed since the events in them. If they need to know what's happening right this second, they can watch CNN. On TV there's one of those reality shows where a pro nanny comes into a troubled family and helps the parents figure out how to keep their horrible kids in line. One of the kids just threw a brick at the nanny. The mom's crying but the nanny doesn't flinch.

I turn down the volume and scan the headlines. It's hard to find anything I can bear to read. The world is falling apart. Whole chunks are crumbling, like one of those medieval maps where the world ends and shit just drops off the side to get eaten by a sea monster.

Maps. Where are you?

I swap the newspaper for my laptop and return to the search. Think logically. If they're coming tomorrow they'll be close. So I start at the dock in Portsmouth where the boats come in from Appledore and Swan, and move inland from there. There are plenty of people out, taking advantage of the hot night and late sunset, shopping in cutesy New England boutiques, eating at tables on the sidewalks. Their bodies are stiff, caught in motion like the corpses preserved in the Pompeii ash, doing normal things just before a disaster, eating, paying the check in a restaurant, pushing a stroller, tugging the arm of a straggling toddler.

I think about the kids that people my age are having, or will start having soon. Life is going to be so boring for them. Not just because the world will have gone completely to shit by then and there won't be much of anything left, but because their parents are going to talk constantly about how the world used to be. Remember when you could just get in your car if you needed to get some-where? Or take a bus or a train even? Remember when everything used to be so much faster? Remember the internet? God, the internet! Remember real meat? Remember fish? I remember when I had my own house for a while. All this space, electricity all the time, taps that turned on and off. No lines for water. No lines for food. Wars all far away. Remember?

Yeah, that'll get dull *real* quick.

It reminds me of this short story. "All Summer in a Day." There was this little girl—wait, I should say first that the story takes place on a human colony on Venus, I think. It rains there all the time; the sun only comes out for an hour every seven years. But the kids who were born there are all used to it; they haven't ever seen the sun, so they don't miss it. Except there's this one girl who's new. Her parents have just moved the family to Jupiter or Venus or wherever and she remembers sunny days from her earthling childhood. But when she goes on and on about how nice life was on Earth, none of the Venus kids understand. She writes all this lovely sunshine poetry and gets all put out because no one gives a shit. Finally the sunny day comes, and she's kind of psychotic looking forward to it, but the asshole other kids lock her in a closet for the whole hour the sun's out and she misses it, which is pretty brutal, and you're obviously supposed to feel sorry for her. And I do, kind of. Someone should have told her not to be such a pain in the ass, though.

The kids that come after my generation will probably get so fed up they'll revolt. They'll be much tougher than we are. I bet by the time they're eleven or so, they'll just slash the shit out of us. Kids'll eat their folks, and with their mouths full they'll parrot their parents talking about *real meat*. I'm not saying it serves them right, just that if you're honest about what people are like, it's understandable. People who don't know how to keep their mouths shut always get fucked with.

Skulking west down all the roads from Portsmouth Harbor, up to the town limit, back down around the green, single-click stubby dead-end streets and halting culs-de-sac. My eyes are sore. I look away from the screen for a few minutes, hold up my finger and alternate my gaze between it and the wall beyond, roll my eyeballs under the lids ten times in each direction. Blink hard. I can't believe I'm still here.

This is no good. Google Earth's imagery runs on a delay, so there's every chance I'm looking too far back in time and they're not there yet. I need to look in real time. Change tack, browser window, search the networked cameras nearby. Hardly anyone bothers to change from the factory default passwords, and they're all online. You don't even need to go through the dark web. A few clicks and you're in. I start at the top of the list and work my way down.

In the low sun, a man's face glows green through the cheap security camera, staring into space like an idiot while he fills his gas tank, kids strapped down in the back seat, each on their own Nintendo DS. He pays at the pump while another guy inside buys a quart of something (windshield-wiper fluid or motor oil maybe) and palms a pack of gum at the checkout. Most people who steal don't really need to, and people who don't need to steal never get caught. A lady in a fur coat fills up a shopping cart in one of those warehouse-size liquor stores. The parking lot camera shows her tipping the kid who had been stocking the shelves a few minutes earlier for loading her bags into a car with out-of-state plates.

Weird thoughts keep popping into my head, so fast I can't keep track of them or try to figure out what they mean. I go out through the kitchen door onto what's left of the backyard and turn away from the water, shiny and black like an oil slick without the rainbow. I lie on my back and look at the show-off spread of clouds. I count the stars in a slow, steady rhythm. My breathing falls in line with my counting, and I go on like this until it's too beautiful and the number's too big for me to be able to think anything in particular.

Tonight's a bit of a nothing moon. Not a half or a sliver. Not full or new, not really, really big or orange-tinted. There are no wicked-witch clouds shuffling across it. It's just a moon that was full a few days ago. The black water slaps its side against the cliffs. I give my mind over to the waves that never tire of the same old dance moves. The cliff and the ocean, a mosh pit of two.

When my skin cools off and goose bumps start to form under the dried sweat I head back inside. The paper's still open on the couch. Dead black men, white-collar criminals getting off with a fine, a drone attack incinerates a wedding, an op-ed piece declaring an end to the age of "isms." *Goodbye racism, sexism, feminism; the world is all grown up and sooo over it!* I close the newspaper and flip through the channels until I find a gentle documentary about religious cults in Japan, settle in, tuck my feet under my legs, and pull the blanket off the back of the couch over my shoulders, more for comfort than warmth.

Just then there's a jolt, hard like repo men kicking down the door. I sit up straight and look around, but no one's there. Everything is still for another second but after that moment it starts again and I realize that it's me, my body shunting with the shock of the noise coming from the cliff outside. The sea is trying to break me. It got sick of slapping and it's punching now, hurling its side against the cliff, pulling back to get its breath before banging, pounding its body, slinging slimy arms up the cliff, trying to pull my house down.

This is one of those moments when you can feel your eyelashes brushing your cheeks and you feel so alone you don't know what to do. At first you can't even scream, but you try again and scream and scream out at the tide pushing against your life and it doesn't give a shit about the fact that you're alone and no one's coming back to save you. You're alone with your voice and the noise and the nothing, nothing but the terrible rest of your life, laying out to mock and taunt you, and there's no one to help.

The monster roars at me; there's nothing in the air but the noise. It's like thunder shouting in my ear, rock and rubble smashing into each other and crashing into the sea below. My muscles grip my bones. This could be it, my house falling down, finally, once and for all. I grip the blanket, force my eyes closed, and wait, listening to the shout and smash of the land falling.

Then nothing for a long time except the gulls and the wind and the waves.

I consider going to the window to see how much land I've lost this time. It's hard to tell if what keeps me inside is fear or resignation, but I guess it doesn't matter. If my house falls down tonight I'll be tucked into my bed when it happens. The guest bed, I mean.

On my way up, something catches my eye from the top of the stairs. A crack all the way down the far wall of the house, from the ceiling to the foundation. It splits a few feet above the floor. It looks like a huge man, standing angry, in my house. He's the slice that lets air through in a sharp, pernicious whistle. Already, mosquitoes are invading through his belly and between his legs. And it's clear he's going to grow.

They have to come tomorrow. I can't stay here.

CHAPTER SIX

Morning tiptoed in while I was sitting up in bed, looking down at the live-streamed world. People carry their shoes along their walks of shame, sometimes stopping to retch in a trash can or the gutter; video baby monitors catch weary parents impatiently scooping crying children from behind the bars of their cribs, trying and failing to bounce them into another hour of sleep; the milk in someone's fridge expired yesterday; rats scurry and scratch and fuck in some kind of warehouse.

The island coos, playing innocent. Gentle swells lap the shore; diffused light drifts through the window. I listen, hard, until I make my ears tickle with the strain. But no matter how hard I listen, the phone still doesn't ring. The only thing I can hear is my stomach rumbling. Acid fumes rise up and bathe the back of my throat. I finished my pie yesterday and didn't bother with dinner after Jason left. I'm going to have to make something. And I know exactly what. The perfection and sadness of it cancel each other out and I feel pretty neutral as I abandon my laptop, roll over onto the floor, and crawl to the stairs, roll down them in a tumbly ball, and walk into the kitchen. The fall hurts just enough.

Eggs out of the fridge to come up to room temperature, butter in a large bowl over the vents at the back of the stove, oven preheated to 350 degrees, flour sifted with a teaspoon of baking powder per cup. One cup of butter, two cups of sugar, three cups of flour, four eggs.

It was a slave recipe that came down from my great-grandmother. My mom said that their recipes had to be simple because they weren't allowed to learn to read. Not really an issue with cooking. Everybody can do that. Baking is all proportions and reactions and ratios. My mom always said that people who can't cook are never really smart, never real adults. It was years before I gave this enough thought to realize that she was probably completely wrong about this. There's probably no relationship between intelligence and cooking either way. She was wrong about lots of things, but I was only six or something and I didn't know that then. Parents aren't really that old. They don't really know anything yet.

When my finger pokes easily into the butter I add the sugar and beat it until the mixture is pale lemon yellow and bubbly. Lick the beaters and then turn the mixer back on to add the eggs one by one. Fold in the flour, gently at first until I get bored and dump the rest in. "One third at a time. Don't get impatient with it. You'll get a sad streak." That's what my mother would say.

Into the oven until you can smell it from the living room. Tiptoe, never peek. She forced me to develop a sense for it, to know, just know. I always meant to time it but never remembered. When I open the oven the top has a lightning bolt crack and bounces back when I press it. While it cools, I beat a pound of butter with a pound of confectioners' sugar and a tablespoon of vanilla. I make myself wait—*learn to be patient*—a whole hour, a little more than an hour, before I frost my cake. In the little utility room behind the kitchen there are some sad little candles in the bottom of one of Lolly's drawers, mostly broken or half burnt, but there's a blue one that's still in pretty good shape, so I take it out, stick it in the middle, and light it. But I don't sing to myself and blow it out or anything stupid like that. I just watch it burn down. It doesn't take that long. I take out a knife and cut myself a slice. Perfect crumb. So much for your compulsive folding, Mother. Only I don't feel like eating anymore, so I slot the slice back into its place, take it outside, plate and all, and throw it off the stupid cliff.

Everyone was born. Who gives a shit.

CHAPTER SEVEN

After last night's landslip the backyard's taken on a half-moon shape as if the sea took an actual bite out of it. Almost noon and the heat is like a boxer, heavy but fast and violent in the air.

There's one particular rock close to the edge—flat and broad, barely visible above the line of the grass—just before the ground goes hollow, where it's really just an overbite with everything underneath already gone. When I squint I can see the heat blurring just above its surface. There might not be enough cliff underneath to support my weight, but I'm drawn to it. I crawl, super low to the ground, more like a snake than a baby, and pile my body on. I relax against the searing stone. It's the perfect size, practically made for me. As I slide out of my T-shirt and underwear, the sun is so hot my skin turns to scales and my blood burns and my bones toast. The light and heat penetrate the density of my hair and sting my scalp and summon up itchy, prickling sweat. I let the heat in under my arms and between my toes. I open my pussy and let the light get as far inside me as it can reach. It's noon up my nose and in my lungs and the ocean can have me if it wants me. Everything can end if it ends like this.

When I can't stand the burning any longer, I go over to the honeysuckle clinging to the front of the house, piggybacked on the five-finger ivy. I pick a flower, pull out the stamen, and let the honey drop on my tongue. A really stupid thought pops into my head: flowers taste better than boys. I'm such an idiot, but for once that thought doesn't get me down. It's so hot. My skin tingles hard, like a violin string, like the surface of a drum. There must be music coming off of me. Maybe I can just stay here forever. It might not be that long.

I think I hear the phone ring, and I freeze, ready to sprint inside, but it's just one of those noises my brain makes.

I settle back onto the rock and stare out at the ocean. It's not so bad right now.

I have a hard time thinking about *a* wave. Like, a single wave. I see them as more a *they* than an *it*. They're beasts, a school of them. A swarm. They move with one brain for a common purpose, making more waves.

The tide's gone in, gentle, orderly, diligent. The waves are Japanese. Their shape is just how they look in prints and on plates; they were definitely invented overseas. The perfection in the way they roll, many in a single unit. Orderly as time, the back pushing its way over to the front. Life went and got perfect, literally a couple of minutes ago, and maybe it'll stay like this for a while, maybe all day even, but I've never been as lucky as that.

———

It's uphill most of the way west to the garden. I have a pair of Lolly's khaki shorts strapped on with a patent leather belt, which, thankfully, my T-shirt hides. Maybe I get too caught up in thinking about times I put my foot in my mouth or about the Swans who are shitty to me. I'm probably being too sensitive. Most of them don't mind me being here too much; being a little cold to me is just part of it. They know I'm a valuable object in the Bad Place: my energy, my health, my body and face. I have a lifetime ahead of me of buying shit made by slaves and then shipped around the world to be bought by wage slaves. When the army recruiters and traffickers and groomers do their rounds, I'm the one they're looking for. Everything to envy and everything to pity about me, these are the things people worship in the Bad Place. I'd reject it too if I was old enough. Instead of taking it personally, I might as well put my difference to good use.

The garden sits on a little plateau, about the size of a decent city playground. There's a greenhouse at the end banged together from materials scavenged from a few ruins around the Shoals. A few yards beyond that are the solar panel and the pump attached to it that brings in seawater and filters out the salt. An army-green rain barrel punctuates the end of each row of raised beds, all heaving with leaves and vines and flowers.

To my left, at the inland side of the garden, the three blond Swans sit at a table they've set up in the shade of a handful of blossoming apple trees. As I approach, I notice their knees are red or smudged with dirt, their faces pink and fixed on fans of playing cards. Their elegant bones pick and rearrange their cards like tidy bouquets.

Grace extends an arm, long and freckled in a yellow sleeveless top, to put down a card. "My zucchinis are unstoppable this year."

"You deserve a good year," Ruth says, taking up three cards from the table, "after last year's massacre."

Grace flutters her hand of cards in Agata's direction. "It's the coffee grounds. Fantastic tip. I mean, they just won't *stop*. Joanna thinks I'm unloading so many zucchinis on her as some kind of prurient joke!"

Grace and Joanna are kind of paired in the unwritten buddy system of food production on the island. There are few enough of them that no one has to keep track. Anyone who doesn't work in the garden has to get their vegetables from someone who does. This means the Wrinklies who *can't* will have veggies hand delivered fresh from the garden, almost every day in the summer, and anyone who's busy with other projects or just can't be bothered has to hand over cash in Rose's shop. Rose supposedly calculates the market rate according to how well each crop is doing, but I think she mostly goes by what she knows everyone can afford to pay. It's different with me because I don't have the same claim to the land that they do. I didn't have to do any of the initial heavy work getting it set up, or pay for the desalination system or build the greenhouse. So I pitch in, and Rose charges me next to nothing in the shop, which is a real lifesaver.

Agata plays two cards. "I swear it's the best thing for keeping slugs away. You know"—she leans her strawberry head toward the others conspiratorially—"this woman told me about using coffee grounds in compost when I was working my community garden project in Detroit. This poor thing, prostitute on crack or meth or God knows what, seven children running around. Well, she knew absolutely all the tricks. Greenest thumbs I've ever seen."

They all make noises like they're *so* impressed that an idiot junkie actually knew something. It's weird how people make fun of drug addicts in a way that they would never make fun of other kinds of disabled people. I guess they think addicts do drugs like they do, all selfish and jolly, like it's fun for them, like addicts live in a massive imaginary nightclub where it's always the weekend and they're having a jamboree. As if it doesn't occur to addicts that they can *just stop.* They look at people suffering and see people partying.

"Now we approach the annual nightmare of endless zucchini peeling," Grace drawls, sounding almost British.

"You *peel* zucchini?" It's a relief to hear Agata say what I was just thinking.

"Everyone peels zucchini."

"No one peels zucchini. Why would you peel zucchini?"

All three are still putting down and taking up cards, but Ruth seems to be taking advantage of the distraction the other two are indulging over vegetable prep.

"It takes out the bitterness."

"It does not."

"It does too. Earl, you peel zucchini, don't you?" The way Grace says *Earl* kind of sounds like a car swerving hard into a U-turn.

"Sure, when I'm making raw pasta, you mean?"

"No, before you cook it, you peel it, right?"

"Why would you peel zucchini?"

Grace puts her cards down in her lap. "You mean that I've spent nigh on three-quarters of a century *peeling* zucchinis to no end whatsoever?"

The question hangs for a bit, and they all laugh.

Earl's putting some tools away, so I ask him what he needs help with.

"Well." He takes a long pause and looks out across the garden. "The compost heap could use a turn, and the two beds on the far left, see, those two at the end? They need a bit of weeding. Think you can handle that?"

He gives me a rough pat on the shoulder like he's the coach and I'm the quarterback.

I grab some gloves and the pitchfork and hike out to the compost heap. Its stink is hot and satisfying. I almost drink it. It resists the fork, exhales in my face as I rip it apart and fold it over on itself. Worms panic. Gases rush the atmosphere. My back and arms ache. I work the mound over until I start to feel sick and realize I forgot to eat again.

I wonder for a second where everyone else is, before remembering that they mostly avoid gardening in the early afternoon. But I think that advice is just for old people and white people. The blondes are in the shade, probably waiting until later to start again. As I return to put down the pitchfork, the telltale coconut scent coming from Earl's deep brown skin reminds me that I really should start wearing sunblock, but I always forget.

Weeding is next, which should be a breeze compared to turning the compost. But once I reach the beds, I'm not sure these are the ones Earl meant. I bend down to look, get onto my hands and knees to push back the leaves of a big lettuce so I can see underneath.

Before I know it, there's a noise that lifts my eyes up. There's a figure charging toward me out from the shade by the trees and the sheds. It's running, waving. Nick, running at me like I really am the quarterback and he's on the other team.

"What are you doing, you idiot? Stop, you idiot! You *idiot*!"

I rise to my knees and look down at my hands, barely able to choke up a flimsy, "What?"

"What are you *doing*?" His face and arms are red like the cartoon villain in an antacid commercial.

"What do you mean?" I really don't know what he's talking about. "Earl asked me to weed the—"

"Those aren't *weeds*. Ugh, *moron*! These are my radish seedlings! They're just starting to come up!"

"But I didn't . . . I was just trying to see . . ."

"Just get away from them. Jesus!"

"They're fine, I swear. I was just confused because . . ."

But the festering boil on two sunburned legs won't even let me explain. Instead he mocks me. "*I was confused*. So, we're all supposed to starve because some dumb little girl is *confused*. Why don't you take your bright ideas and inexperience and ineptitude back to the Bad Place and launch a start-up?"

He drops to his knees to survey the damage, still muttering *goddamn* this and *fucking* that and insulting me, failing to notice that he's having a fit over nothing. He'll probably find his radishes coming up in a couple of weeks and think that he saved them from me. I just want to slink away and hide. I want to say sorry to everyone for everything. I'm exposed—the sun is high and hot, everyone is peering at me from their shelter in the shade—and I'm probably the least likely to die today but I'm craving it badly now, burning for it.

Taking up my tools and gloves, I feel as shaken as if I'd just been in a fight. I just want my mom and dad to come get me. That's all I want. The thought seems to slice the inside of my forehead and I have to grimace it away or it'll make me cry as I walk back toward all these faces, now settling into the games or chores, but still taking glances at me with bystanders' expressions.

Earl has joined the blondes' game of rummy, and Helen and Nancy have arrived and taken his place in the shade by the shed, poking their fingers into trays of soil on the long wooden table and sprinkling seeds into the holes.

"So, I meant the beds on the left facing seaward, not looking inland from the far end," Earl offers gently as I heft the mixture of hydrogen peroxide and water out of the shed to clean the pitchfork.

"I would have figured—" I was going to say that I would have figured it out, that I could tell I didn't have it right, but they're all looking at me or kind of tutting.

And then Nancy chimes in, trying to be helpful, changing the subject. "Couldn't be any worse than the number the mice pulled on my onion bulbs."

"Store them in gravel; that'll keep the mice out," Agata offers.

"And they don't germinate?" Ruth asks.

"Mine never do."

"Funny we still get these occasional bursts in mouse activity, way out here. Must be strong swimmers!" Grace says in a half giggle.

"Stowaways." That's Nick, back from rescuing his ravished crop. I try to work faster without doing a half-assed job and having someone yell at me again. "They make their way out here, bed down, make their nests real nice and cozy. Even an island won't keep pests out completely." He gives me a pointed look.

After an embarrassed pause, Ruth makes a play and wins the hand. Earl notices that the sun has shifted and pulls his basket of vegetables over into the shade while Grace deals again. She calls to me as I turn to leave. "Going already?"

"Yeah." I could use this opening to explain, but I'm afraid if I bring it up, everyone will just start interrupting me again, and if I get any more frustrated I'll lose it completely. "Yeah, I have to . . . emails. Loads of emails to deal with . . ."

She smiles underneath her shielded eyes; her seat is in the sun now, too. "Good to see you out in the garden. Green is good for the eyes."

I smile to thank her and she meets my eye for a moment before she takes up her hand of cards and starts arranging. I can feel Nick glaring but I hold in tears until the terrain slopes, forcing my steps into a jog. And even then I only cry a little.

CHAPTER EIGHT

Out of the green and into the dim stillness that hangs in my house, almost the color of smoke. The blue light from my laptop seems to make the living room chilly rather than any brighter. Or maybe I'm just still shaking from the garden. Fuming even. I was just trying to help and that fucking septic hemorrhoid . . . And over *nothing*, seriously nothing at all . . .

I could break his nose. I close my eyes and picture it; my mouth is watering to smash my forehead right into the middle of his fat, wrinkly face. Then he'd shut the fuck up and listen to me. I didn't even touch them. I could have stabbed him with the pitchfork, I could burn his fucking house down . . . Why wouldn't anybody let me explain, not one of them?

"Fuck! Fuck them all!"

I squeeze out a few more tears, practically force them, while I scream, heave, breathe, open a new window, type into the address bar. Enter.

The tool I need takes a few minutes to download onto a memory stick. Meanwhile I try to do some calculations: I probably walk twice as fast as Nick. He's in good shape, but he's pushing a hundred.

So even if he left the garden just after me, I'd still have a few minutes on him. His house is about ten minutes from here, less if I run, though I'd run the risk of him seeing me on the way back. But if he's still at the garden and doesn't leave for another half an hour or so, and if I really bolt . . .

The finder bings and I eject the stick—run out of the house, climb the hill up to the road, run hard against the swelling cramp in my belly until I find my hips square with his front door.

His house is just like mine but further from the cliff. Two stories, simple shingled roof, wooden siding painted white, gray door, and big windows like the neighborhood watch. I keep reminding myself that he's not home. He might be right behind me, though, so I can't afford to hesitate.

Inside it's not what I expected. Chalky beige walls instead of blue-gray. No desk, no bookcases. He must keep his computer in the small room upstairs. The word for his living room is *handsome*. Long brown leather sofa with a pattern made out of tightly sewn-on buttons, matching armchairs, two lamps like the ones in fancier public libraries. No pictures of family, just one long painting of a ye olde nautical battle. It's not so much that it looks clean, but that it doesn't seem like it could ever get dirty or messy, or like the furniture could possibly be arranged any other way. But the smell is disturbing, like when a stranger's car is a little too nice and you regret getting in.

I head upstairs and it's just where I suspected—across the landing from the master bedroom, a newish Dell with a monitor that's older than the computer. I tap the mouse, happy to find the machine on standby. *password. password1. password1234. nicholas1234.*

Password1234 and I'm in. Obviously people who don't even lock their doors are hardly going to do any better with their computers. With a couple of clicks the ProRat tool is installing, bedding in, like a stowaway.

When it's finished, I eject my USB and send his system to sleep so he'll find it just as he left it, push the mouse back to the center of its gray pad, slip out of the study leaving the door ajar, pull his front door behind me carefully but firmly so I can hear it click but no one nearby would hear it slam. And then I have to hold back the temptation to run, forcing myself into long strides in case I bump into someone and need to feign a stroll.

Back at Lolly's house, in the guest room, across the landing from the master bedroom (the same room Nick uses as a study). In terms of layout and structure, the two houses are twins. It looks like my desk in Lolly's guest room is even in the same place as Nick's desk in his study. Ever since I learned how easy it is to hack webcams, I always keep a piece of tape over mine. Not fifteen minutes ago I was in the equivalent room in his house looking at his monitor. Now I'm in the guest room of my grandmother's house, looking at my laptop, through his monitor, and into the same room. It's creepy, looking at my computer screen and seeing a room exactly like the one I'm in but with a different life filling it, like I've just moved again with my parents and forgotten where I am. He has lots of books, hardbacks with dark spines segregated from the bright dwarf paperbacks, and instead of awkward watercolors he displays what looks like framed newspaper articles, maybe ones he won awards for. That annoys me.

I route my IP through a proxy server; better safe than sorry.

Then into the back end of his operating system to run a quick script

```
<!DOCTYPE html>
<html>
<head>
<meta name='viewport' content='initial-scale=1.0, user-scalable=no'>
<meta charset='utf-8'>
<title>Simple Polygon</title>
<style>
/* Always set the map height explicitly to define the size of the div
* element that contains the map. */
#map {
height: 100%;
}
/* Optional: Makes the sample page fill the window. */
html, body {
height: 100%;
margin: 0;
padding: 0;
}
</style>
</head>
<body>
<div id='map'></div>
<script>
```

and wait.

His browser history is predictable. Streams free porn, doesn't download it, online banking, newspapers. Wow, eight thousand Twitter followers and he hardly ever tweets. Googled himself a few days ago and actually got some new hits. But my eyes keep getting drawn to his bookshelf. I can't make out the titles. I think about the lines in my dad's forehead when he's reading. William Gibson, Douglas Adams, Carl Sagan, Clive Barker, Anne Rice, Robert R. McCammon. Usually big, usually hardback, I thought they must be very serious. He didn't keep his books. Maybe he would have if we had ever settled down the way they promised that we would someday. Instead he liked to leave them, abandon them in public. He didn't dog-ear the pages to mark them and was prissy with paperback spines, so they were always in good shape when he'd take in the last sentence and put the book down next to him on the subway or a bench or a diner counter and just walk off. Everybody's secret Santa. I bet he would've liked to have a library, but instead he was Johnny Appleseed sprinkling the country with sci-fi classics and highbrow horror, fantasies of worlds half ending.

The way he can't read when my mother's in the room; his eyes keep sneaking up and tracing her movements. I wonder now if she could always see him looking, if this was another one of their little private games.

I duck when Nick enters the frame and bash my forehead on my desk. God, I even have the reflexes of an idiot. It's eerie being this close to him, face craggy with pores and lines in the unforgiving light of his screen, eyes a breath away from mine, and having him looking into space, unable to see me at all. I know this isn't the same as being brave. It is cunning, though.

For all his expensive furniture, his ergonomics are pretty bad.

I click over and check that the script I planted in his hard drive is running, then ⌘+tab back to his webcam in time to see him jerk his head up and back away from the screen, hold his hand between it and his face, drop his hand, and move his face closer. This dude's nose hairs are *in charge*. Seriously, you could braid them.

He's trying to write an email to his grandson, but keeps stopping and rubbing his eyes. Oh, what's this? Reaching for his glasses, puts them on but . . . no good, is it, Gramps? Now he's getting up; he's gone for a little under a minute. Holy shit, no! Back in his seat, he's got his head tilted back, putting in eye drops. Looks like a little girl made you cry. Oh my God, this is classic. I could watch this all day, Nick trying to read the *New York Times* on-screen, rubbing his eyes, getting up and checking his vision by reading a book (with glasses and without), coming back to his computer where it's clear he can barely make out the words on his display. Whether he gets his eyes fixed or his computer (which has got to be out of warranty), it'll cost him. I'll change it back before he takes it in to be repaired, so the tech guys won't find anything. And because it seems like a hardware fault, they won't even notice that I was ever there.

It's a particularly mean trick to play on a Wrinkly but Nick's also a douche, so they cancel each other out. My parents, for all their piss-poor judgment and honest mistakes, didn't raise me to take shit from bullies. My mother used to say, *It's just us, us against the world*. She said that to me once when I told her I was losing my friends, toward the end of elementary school. I think I was nine—one of those ages when you think things will change soon but nothing does. My dad always said to pick your battles, especially when the other guy's bigger. But if you can fight back, fight dirty; the odds are already stacked against you, so do damage any way you can.

My friends had started to trust me less. I didn't get invited over as much, and no one ever came to my house anymore. I didn't hold it against them. I didn't much like being there either. And I was just a scrawny kid, underweight and geeky and confused.

At the same time, my parents' friends started spending a lot more time at our house. I wondered how they made friends so easily when I always felt like I never knew what to say to people. Their new friends had an odd quality, something I might have complained about to my mother if I could have named it. It was big, like generosity, except the opposite. They all seemed to want something from me. They were so eager to make me smile that I had no choice—forcing giggles at their stupid coin tricks and dumb jokes. These people smelled odd. Acrid, oily. They had greasy skin and angry zits, mouths vandalized with gaps and patches of metal, orange and black clinging to their teeth like the mold and mildew on our bathroom grout, or sludgy brown teeth that looked like they hadn't been inserted right and were slipping out. I couldn't say I hated them because they were ugly, so I held my breath and played along. They'd give me hard pieces of bubble gum and listen so intently to the Bazooka Joe comics, laugh so hard at these jokes that were lost on me, but I had to laugh too. It was like I was quenching something in them. They scratched instant-win lotto tickets and sometimes won a dollar. They liked to stay up late. I remember how I pressed my face into my pillow, waiting for them to pass out and the noise to clear and the sun to come up and send them hiding.

Lolly was around a lot more then too, so it must have been while we were living in Boston. She'd come sometimes on the weekends. There was a mother-daughter softball game and Lolly took me, and she bought ice cream for everyone, and even my friends who'd known me through elementary school seemed happy to think of her as my mom. It made me feel wrong, being there with her instead of my mother, and I put my ice cream in a bush when no one was looking. She took me to the award dinner for an essay contest I'd entered. I won third prize. My parents couldn't come for some reason. Maybe the hotel was too far away and they didn't have a car.

————

Dad left us once. I don't remember when he left exactly or how long he stayed away, but I can remember him not being there. Parents don't ask kids before they move the furniture or paper over the walls. You just walk in one day and the house you live in is different. Could it really have been as casual as that? I can't remember. One afternoon I was watching TV after school and the phone rang. It was a collect call, but different. An automated voice said, *You have a collect call from Northeastern Correctional Center. If you do not wish to accept this call, HANG UP.* The force of those last two words . . . my father didn't deserve that. The word *criminal* started to feel different. He came on after I accepted the charge. I wanted to say something to make it okay for him, but trying to talk was like being forced to eat glass. He sounded uneasy too, never settling on one subject for very long, not responding directly to anything that I said. Pretty quickly he asked to speak to my mother, who took the phone into another room. We never talked about it. Why didn't anyone ever just tell me what was going on? Don't prisoners' families visit them, in movies and on TV? It was like they thought I wouldn't notice he was gone. No, it was that they trusted I knew how to keep my mouth shut when it mattered.

Then there was the night of the boxing match. Dad had been back for a few days or maybe a week. The night smelled like the smoke that comes off a wooden match when you drop it in a bottle of beer. Steam, sulfur, alcohol. Everyone was excited. I don't re-member how many people were over but it felt crowded. In my memory everyone is wearing short sleeves or tank tops, and has round biceps and long forearms, but that can't be right. The air was hot and sticky and sour. The carpet felt damp, oversoft. I wanted to go home. But I was home.

Everyone put a dollar in a soft, old baseball cap. I guess the people who chose the right boxer to win got to split the money. My dad gave me a dollar and let me put it in. We watched everything—all the prefight chat, white men in suits going on and on in shouting voices, statistics on the screen. I thought it was all so boring. I wonder why I didn't just leave.

Menthol cigarette butts were crowding the bottom of a green beer bottle on the floor, ash clinging to the neck. I accidentally kicked it over and everyone laughed and pointed. My mother had thick hair under her arms. I could smell it. Yes, she must have been wearing a tank top. No bra. I could see her breasts distinctly, and

I didn't like how they felt on my cheek when she pulled me in for a cuddle. She had bad breath. But I still didn't want her to let go of me.

Then the fight started. Everyone was screaming even though all the boxers had done was walk into the room wearing silly robes with sequins on them like weirdly musclebound wizards. They made their way into the ring while the room became even more claustrophobic with screaming and mentholated smoke. In opposite corners of the ring two black men bounced, both already glistening with sweat. While they threw practice punches into the air and wiped sweat off their faces with their gloves, I checked out the people in the audience. There was a blond woman in the front row with a lot of jewelry. I wished I could get a better look at her but she was mostly obscured by the boxing ring. She was sitting next to a man with a deep orange tan.

No one here can see me.

The bell sounded and the boxers began to circle each other. I didn't understand how they were actually going to do this. It seemed like it would be so easy to dodge a punch in a ring that big. I suppose it didn't occur to me that surviving the fight wasn't the point. After a while my mind started to wander. I watched the strata of smoke in the air, concentrated on the gentle way they hung there. Every time someone leapt up in anger or excitement and broke through my layers of smoke, I hated them; they made them move too fast, disrupted the subtlety by being so brash, jumping through the pretty gray smoke ribbons to scream at the TV like agitated seagulls. Their bodies were made of noise and ash turned to mud with cheap beer.

The fight went on and on, gloves on flesh on bone, fighters clinging to each other like they were so tired they could drop dead. The referee pulled them apart and made them keep fighting. How could this be normal, pleasurable, thrilling even, watching two people burst each other's flesh with the force of their punches? Why was it an occasion for the people on TV to dress up in suits and jewels, and for my parents to throw a party? Why did they all love this misery? Every time the bell rang I crossed my fingers, wishing for it to be over, but the boxers just flopped onto stools in opposite corners, drooling as they pulled out their wet mouth guards. I cringed when their coaches squirted water in their faces and in their mouths. Then the bell and they were back to the center of the ring, bouncing and attacking, crouching, blocking, bleeding gooey ropes from busted lips, then back to their corners, then back to the center again. Finally the one in blue had become a zombie, slick all over as if every part of his body was weeping. His punches stopped connecting and he couldn't block the hits that sent him to the floor. He tried to get up when the referee counted to ten, but it was no use. Everyone was shouting now—some of them cheering in high tones, others flinging long bare arms over disappointed faces. Three . . . two . . . one. The boxer I'd put my money on lost.

I was still upset when my mother put me to bed. She kissed me on my temple and went back down to watch the second fight and I lay in bed and listened. The door of my room was ajar, the clang of the bell and the shouts of the crowd on TV and the crowd downstairs coming to me through the thick gray smoke ribbons lying on the air.

A shape stepped into the slice of light in my doorway; I heard the sound, and the sizzle. And then the smell. Downstairs a few people screamed. Something must have happened in the fight. The shape exhaled a lungful of cigarette smoke and came in. There was a small thud as he put his beer bottle down by the far wall. More screams from below. The smell of the beer-wet cigarette butt was so close now it stung.

I tried to be very still but my eyes were wide open. I thought he wouldn't be able to see them. I don't know why. Then he spoke to me. "I'm sorry you didn't win."

His sweat was oil, grease. What you might sweat if you were a machine. That's what I remember about him, skin so slick with sweat it was too shiny to look at.

The air was so sour as he got closer. He put his hand on my face—it covered almost my entire face, as if to hold me there. His hand smelled like a match. My mouth filled with salt. I wanted my dad to hear me wishing for him, hear me needing him in that moment. But I didn't call him, and he didn't come.

Wait. What is that smell?

I sit up in my chair in Lolly's spare room and the noise comes again. An explosion, not nearby but not super-distant either. Like cannons in historical dramas on TV. I listen for a while and eventually start to wonder if I'd imagined it.

I felt bad for him on Christmas. Dad. I never knew what to get him. December would come around and I couldn't ever think of anything that he might like. Nothing I saw brought him to mind. Nothing ever made me think, Daddy would love that. How lonely. Yeah, I think he was pretty lonely.

The too-harsh bang of the bell to end the round. The smell of booze-sweat and matches—hot matches sizzling at the bottom of a beer bottle. The horrible thud of a boxer's fist on another boxer's face.

And then it happens again. My eyes spring open and my head turns toward the noise—the north side of the island.

I've developed the attention span of a retired person. Easily intrigued, ready to march to the village green or whatever and sniff out trouble. I guess everyone in a small town has this, the need to latch on to anything out of the ordinary. There's no point thinking about it too much. I'm getting old, like everyone else.

CHAPTER NINE

By the dock at the north side of the island, a few Swans are gathered, looking out toward Duck Island, and some other Wrinklies who have been sunbathing on towels are sitting up, pointing or shrugging as they toss a conversation between them. There's something I really like about seeing old people naked, but I'd never tell anyone that. It sounds too weird, though I actually don't see why it should.

Earl seems like a good person to ask what's happening. He's really smart, plus he has a pair of binoculars pressed against the black freckles on his cheeks. I walk up and ask him if he knows what all the noise was about, and I know he hears me, but it takes him ages before he even turns his head in my direction. Then he just does this *I'm really disappointed in you* head shake, and I start to wonder if I should've asked Louise instead.

Earl finally decides to actually say something. "The problem is the methane. We told them. I went over there on Ted's boat. No, it was the schooner, the little schooner that Lyall used to have, but he lost it in a bet. Or he sold it; that's right, sold it to that fellow on Star . . . Eh . . . but I went over there and I *told* 'em . . ."

Okay, I don't mean to be mean or anything, but old people take incredibly. Long. Pauses. They get it back eventually, a second before you start to wonder if they'd notice if you just walked away.

"There was probably a problem with . . . you know . . ."

I *don't* know. I really don't. I touch my pocket to make sure I have my phone. Wouldn't this be the perfect time for my mother to call me? I'd have to take it—no one would think that was rude. My long-lost mother coming back to fetch me. Of course I'd have to take the call.

". . . oh, *you know*."

Jesus, Earl, *no*. I *don't know*.

God, I'm hungry. What time is it? I could pull out my phone and look at the time, but I might as well say, Sir, you are so boring that I have completely given up trying to follow your demented ramblings, and he'd mutter something to Rose and she'd start to lose patience with me and that's my only friend down the drain. I raise my eyebrows, face-language for *Oh, that's so interesting . . .*

"Methane pockets!" Which he says like he's talking about something really awesome but actually he's just stoked to have been able to come up with the word.

"Of course, city hall was looking at near on fifty years of nil revenue from the landfill on the island. Might as well sell it to the Japanese, that's what some folks said. Whole damn island . . ."

Then I'm thinking about sex with Jason, the way guys move when they're having sex with you. Do guys keep their legs together when they have sex to protect their secret vaginas? No, of course they don't. If dudes had vaginas, word would have gotten out a long time ago. They'd have, like, a documentary about it or something. Somebody told me that ducks have lots of vaginas. But that couldn't be right, could it? God, what a weird train of thought.

". . . so for near enough a decade the, ah . . ."

I am so fucking hungry. I could finish that pie when I get back to the house. No, wait, I gave it to Rose yesterday because Nick has the manners of a fascist and can't even take a polite bribe. Shit.

". . . Duck Island was one giant landfill. And all the way out here . . . ah . . . the . . . ah . . . regulatory framework is, you know . . ."

"Yeah. *Totally.*"

"And the stuff some people throw out needs handling a certain way. That's why the regulations are there, not just to give the bean counters more beans to count."

I imagine an assembly line in an old factory in the former USSR. It's gray and the strip lights are blinking and men with mustaches in matching, boxy uniforms are making little lines on paper every time a bean rolls by . . .

". . . which is why my wife only used cloth diapers on our four boys."

Shit, I missed something.

"Not the explosions, of course. I don't reckon we were thinking too much about explosions if I'm going to be perfectly honest with you. But pack them in too tight and pressure . . . it's a . . . ah . . . it's *literally* a ticking time bomb."

I think I also heard that ducks have corkscrew penises. Wait, no way. Whoever told me that was totally fucking with me. Sometimes I'm so gullible it's embarrassing.

"Ya *see?*"

"Yeah, wow . . . Intense."

"Yep, just a matter of time—I *told* 'em . . ."

"Ahoy, Small-fry!" Rose, thank God. "Did Earl get you all filled in?" I nod. "Crazy stuff, huh?"

I nod again.

"So word is they're evacuating Duck, that's what Hazel says."

For the next few minutes I just listen, and from what I'm able to piece together from Rose and Earl gabbing with the other Wrinklies, the explosions on Duck are from illegal trash dumping, like thirty or forty years ago. Portsmouth City used to pay the owner to bury garbage there because their landfill was full, and construction on the new one was running behind. The site out here wasn't set up like a proper landfill (and this is where Earl loses me again, something about checks and standards and regulations and pressure gauges or something) so the trash didn't get buried in the special, nonexplosive way that it usually is. Once the new landfill was finished they stopped the Duck Island operation. Once the island wasn't generating income, the owner covered over the dumping site and sold it cheap to the University of New Hampshire, who set up a marine science research lab there. I don't know why people need to come out to some nowhere island to study fish, but I don't ask because Earl probably knows the answer, *in detail*. So anyway, the problem was disposable diapers. If they get put under too much pressure for years and years, they can just blow up. So now the college kids on Duck have to pack up their stethoscopes or whatever and evacuate or risk getting maimed by the most heinous landmines of all time.

While we're hanging out with Earl still explaining the ins and outs of trash explosions and his late wife's mothering philosophies, and how they hitchhiked to Woodstock from Vermont when she was pretty much ready to pop out her second ankle-biter, and he had the first one strapped to the front of his overalls, the boat from Duck leaves its moorings and bobs over the waves toward Swan. The idea of a small boatload of brainy college dudes rocking up here doesn't bother *me*, but when they do that tossing-the-rope-on-the-pier thing sailors always do, the Swans are *not* having it.

Frances and Gretchen have come down from the Oceanic, and by now most of the Swans have assembled on the beach. One of the sunbathers starts to get up and puts a towel on, but seeing how the others stay where they are, naked and wrinkly and proud, she gets back down on her towel. She looks embarrassed, though, and that makes me pissed off at the kids on the boat, too.

So anyway, an older dude (older in mainland terms—like forty or something) hops off and approaches Frances and Gretchen on the dock. After a couple of minutes they come down to confer with Mrs. Tyburn and Giddy. The dude from Duck starts waving his arms around and pointing at the island. Another antique diaper blows a thick, soft-edged column of brown-gray smoke into the air; he points over and goes, *See?* like we didn't see the six or seven that happened earlier, like we always just stand here staring at Duck Island in the afternoon.

Mrs. Tyburn, Giddy, Frances, and Gretchen walk him back to the dock, kind of half pushing him like bouncers. It's pretty awesome. I move closer to the dock to listen in. Rose comes too. It seems like they're letting Mrs. Tyburn do all the talking, which is appropriate, seeing as she always acts like she owns the place.

"We're not unsympathetic, this much I'm sure you understand. But you simply must respect the basic rules of our community."

The Swans are getting restless. "Take it to Star!"

"Thank you, Grover." Mrs. Tyburn smiles at Grover, the island hobo. He's really a retired investment banker, but he always wanted to be a hobo when he was a boy growing up in a fancy house, so on Swan he lives in a tent on an inlet on the north side and eats out of tin cans with a rusty old spoon.

Mrs. Tyburn goes on: "Yes, I'm sure they can spare some fresh water and camping space for the night on Star Island until you're able to make meaningful contact with your university."

I guess they wanted to stay here on account of all the extra rooms in the Oceanic.

"Shove off, smooth face!" Earl shouts.

"Go back to the Bad Place!" Giddy adds.

"What about her?" the science guy asks. He's looking at me. Obviously.

"None of your business!" Grover yells.

"Special dispensation," Mrs. Tyburn says.

"She's not staying."

That was Rose.

So they pull up their anchor. They probably don't really have an anchor. It's probably just an expression. All the Swans stand there and watch until they get to the dock at Star. I watch too because I don't know where else to look.

Then there are hands on my shoulders. "Come on, Small-fry."

I walk back to the shop with Rose. The bells chime when we walk in. And my stomach grumbles.

"Did any mail come today?"

"Nothing for you today."

Rose's cane is over by the fruit.

"Can I get a chicken, please, Rose?"

"Sparky?" Sparky's the smallest.

"Actually, I think I'll have Calvin."

Rose takes her shears down from their hook on the wall, I get the knife from the crate under the counter, and we walk through the shop to her backyard, stopping in the kitchen on our way out so I can put a big pot of water on to boil. I find Calvin, all red and quick, trying to steal whatever the other chickens are pecking. When he sees me coming, he does that chicken jog, changing directions really fast, and I feel stupid chasing him in front of Rose. She's laughing at me while she clips some tarragon in the herb patch, which is obviously really helpful. She's much better than I am at this, but she always makes me do it myself. She says it's good for me. She's probably right but it's a fucking pain in the ass.

I stop and act casual until Calvin relaxes and gets back to bullying the others. He's not close, but I can tell he's forgotten about me, so I lunge and get him by one of his legs. And of course he's flapping and struggling hard, trying to pull his body away, but I position him in my arms and pull him into my body. I take him over to the bench where I've left the knife, sit him in my lap, and pet him. And when he's nice and calm I say thank you, like Rose taught me to, find the place where his jaw meets his beak, place the knife in a tiny gap between feathers directly against his skin, and cut his throat. The knife is sharp; the only thing that could prevent it from slipping easily through the slim column of skin and tendon and muscle and organs is doubt. Hesitation causes unnecessary suffering at moments like these, so you have to cut with complete conviction or not at all. He's completely still for a second while gooey red blood spits onto the grass in a stream the thickness of a nickel. Then his body spasms and his wings try to flap, but I've got him hard on my lap. And when his body is still again I take his head and pull it back, breaking his neck, and with a final twist pull off his head.

I hoist the pot of steaming water off the stove and into the yard and dip the carcass into it by its scaly feet. After a few seconds in the water, I loop a length of twine around one of the feet, hang it from a low tree branch, and start pulling the sodden feathers away from the bumpy skin. Rose comes over and hands me a burlap bag.

"Sorry." I've forgotten to bring it out and the feathers are starting to make a mess.

"It's all right, junior. Just pay more attention next time."

Rose does all this for the Swans but not for me. Which is fine. I kind of like doing it. Not in a serial-killer way. It just makes me feel like I can take care of myself. And the exposed skin, the swollen dotted lines that cover it—it feels like something I have to face up to.

"So you've been mouthing off to Mrs. Tyburn . . ."

"What'd I say?"

"You called her Cruella de Vil. To her face."

"She killed a bee." Rose appears unmoved. "They're endangered!"

Rose takes a deep breath in, like she's about to lay some heavy shit on me, even though I totally already know what she's going to say. "Mind you, you're a *guest* here. And Mrs. Tyburn's peculiar project keeps you in chicken and pie. Keeps body and soul together."

Something about that last thing strikes me as funny.

"So I'll thank you to mind yer Ps and Qs, if it doesn't inconvenience you terribly, mad-moi-zelle."

"Yes, ma'am." That's what she likes to hear when she's *giving me a talking-to*.

"That's more like it." She does her head-tilty smile like she's satisfied. "*So*, Calvin, eh? Dinner for two?" See, I usually get the smallest chicken in the, like, herd, or whatever you call it when it's chickens. "Jason stay over?"

"My parents are coming for me today."

"Tap my feet and call me Bojangles! They called!"

"Well, no. That's why I know they're coming today. I mean, if they haven't called that means they're just going to rock up, like a surprise. I mean, if they get the late boat out to Appledore, they could probably . . ."

She does a squint-frown; she doesn't understand. And something in her expression makes what I was saying stop making sense to me too.

"It's my birthday. I'm eighteen."

Rose gives a big "aww" and hugs me, which sends loads of Calvin's feathers flying. And then it looks like she wishes she didn't get up so fast and she has to grab the back of the bench and lower herself back down.

"You doing anything nice?"

"I made a cake."

"And you didn't bring me any?"

"I'm a growing girl."

"*Woman*. That's what you say now. Ya hear?"

"Yes, ma'am." I pull the last of Calvin's feathers off his wings and turn him around and around, tugging off the stragglers.

"Right!" and she slaps her hand down on the counter in her *yee-haw* way. "What d'you say I take you out to the Relic tonight?"

"The Relic? Will they even let me in? Nick would go apeshit."

"You leave that to ol' Rose." She goes on, but now she sounds a little unsure, like she's speaking a foreign language. "Bring yer folks."

"Yeah. I will. Sounds good."

All naked like this, Calvin just seems like chicken as opposed to *a* chicken—a real animal with a personality and shit. Rose looks him over and smiles at my work. I follow her inside and into her kitchen, feeling eager to show Rose that I know what to do next. I slice an opening midway between the thighs, reach in and pull out his guts, cut the heart away from the lungs, remove the kidneys and the liver, discard the intestines and stomach into the white plastic bin. The organ meat goes into a little plastic bag and back down into the cavity. I wrap the chicken up in paper, wash my hands, give the countertop a good scrub, and remember to say thank you to Rose.

She hands me a bunch of tarragon tied up with twine. I reach into my pocket and she leans over and slaps my hand. Her rings sting but I know she didn't mean them to. "No, ma'am, not today you don't pay. Not for one thing, ya hear?"

"Thanks, Rose. Really."

"You're welcome, Small-fry. See you around sunset."

———

Someone's ringing the chapel bell. Every once in a while there'll be talk about buying a thing you could set to make the bell ring on the hour, which seems like it would be really nice actually. But a lot of the Wrinklies thought it would be dodgy having a machine keeping time, and I can see their point, too. But leaving it up to the Swans was a massive fail. When they tried to work out a system of people coming and ringing the bell themselves it fell apart pretty quickly. That's what Rose told me. Wrinklies would show up late or miss a shift altogether and people kept getting confused about what time it was. After a couple of days no one was using it to tell the time anyway, so they decided it was pointless to try, and let it drop. Since everyone likes the bell, people just ring it whenever they feel like it. And they ring it before island meetings, but they're not having one today, they're having one tomorrow—the meeting to talk about the Duchess—so right now it's just someone ringing the bell for the hell of it. It doesn't mean anything.

I listen to it anyway. I wish I'd started counting the tolls right away. Probably six so far. I head for the center and climb the rocky path that leads up to the chapel and keep counting. Seven more. The grass brushes my legs and as I approach the chapel it feels like I'm walking up to a big, friendly, sleepy animal. Maybe it appeals to me so much because it's right in the middle of the island. If you're looking at the chapel, you can't see the ocean. It's the one exception, the one place where you can feel safe from the sea. But if I corrected the Swans every time they pulled their whole "Have you noticed that you can see the ocean from every point in the island?" routine, I'd seem like a smart-ass. Or, what's that thing Rose is always calling me? Contrary.

There are people inside talking so I don't go in. I think it's the quilting group. I decide to go to the Oceanic for a bit.

Joanna and Ernie wave at me as I make my way up the stairs, and when I get closer I can hear them talking about Duck. Apparently there are still people down on the beach watching the explosions, which are happening less often, but there's still the occasional thud.

There are more flowers in the Duchess's room today, plants from the greenhouse. One contingent says it's wasteful to grow anything that's purely decorative since there's only a small space to grow things on the island; people like Nick who say, "We don't have capacity to carry passengers." Since the Duchess has been bedridden, more of the garden and greenhouse space has been taken up by flowers that are just flowers for flowers' sake. So there.

There's a new orchid that must have been smuggled in from the Bad Place. I can't imagine anyone growing something like that here. An orchid will die in such a sunny room, but I guess it'll outlive the Duchess. A dead orchid would look pathetic—bent, empty twig of a stem, any flowers that managed to hang on curled and limp like cold French fries—and even though this one looks okay right now, I know what's going to happen eventually, and that makes it hard to look at, so I put it on the floor by the dresser on the other side of the room. There's a pot of bushy flowers with yellow middles and three white leaves on each blossom sitting on the book we were reading, and now the cover's all bloated from water draining out of the bottom, and the edges of the pages are stained.

I know she isn't going to get better, but I still listen hard to the rhythms of the machines that mime her life for her. I watch her closed eyes and try to read the movement beneath her eyelids.

But it's not Morse code. It doesn't mean anything.

I hear footsteps and pick up the book. The cover is soggy and I don't like holding it. And I don't understand the guilty feeling in my stomach. I was just watching her. She's my friend as much as theirs. I wasn't doing anything wrong. Except maybe wanting her to stay here with me. I feel guilty for being selfish.

I think of us as climates constantly threatened by storms that always break somewhere else. The empty immensity of things, the great forgetting that fills sky and earth . . .

Between words I listen to the machines breathing for the Duchess's body, pushing air in and pulling it out again. Her heart beats a pulsing LED landscape. Her blood is a single red line.

"God, I'm so tired, Dutch. I slept all morning and I'm still so tired. It should be me. I should be you and you should be me. The one of us who wants a life should have it. It should be me in that bed. I don't know what to do."

She'd know what to do, if she still had a mind to know things. I know this in my heart as another dull thud comes blasting out of Duck.

I'm about to start reading again when I get an odd, urgent sense that it's time to go. I put my lips to the soft, worn skin on the Duchess's forehead and leave her to the flowers and machines. As I make my way down the stairs, it becomes clear that one of the voices I hear is familiar but out of place. I slip a little but manage not to stumble down the steps. My heart speeds up like I'm running or falling. But . . . no. It's not my dad.

It's coming from one of the rooms they use for checkups and treatments and stuff like that. "Tee, oh, zee."

Shit, it's Nick. I hide my smile behind my palms and hang back away from the door.

"Good," Gretchen coos in her reassuring doctor way. "Line four?"

"L, P, E, D . . ."

"And nothing else is going on? No headaches? Spots in your vision?"

"No, nothing."

"What about phantom smells, nausea, anything like that? Sleeping more than usual?"

"For Christ's sake, I told you, everything else is completely normal."

He doesn't have to shout at her. Listening to him snarking is killing my satisfaction-high. I try to sneak by, but I'm only just past the door when I can feel eyes on me. I can sense her looking before she says anything, and I know it's going to be a massive pain in the ass but there's no way to escape.

It's Gretchen, obviously. "Can we talk for a minute?"

"Me? Aren't you busy with a patient?"

Nick comes out of the examination room behind her. "We're

done here." And he walks out without thanking her or anything. Douche.

Gretchen looks back at me. "Five minutes?"

The weight of the bag in my hand gets my attention. "I have a chicken here. From Rose. I'd better get home, get it in the fridge."

"Here." She reaches out and takes it from me. Just takes it. "I'll stick it in ours. Go have a seat in my office."

It's more of an order than an invitation. I do as I'm told. Just my shit luck—marooned on a secluded island with no parents and instead of getting to do whatever I want I've got a zillion old grand-dorks bossing me around.

Gretchen's office is okay I guess. It's decorated in the antiquey style that Mrs. Tyburn uses in her house, but there's less stuff. Hardly any ornaments. Leather-bound books with serious titles line up in a dark wood bookcase. A desk, a lamp with glass tiles forming a flower-shaped shade, a framed picture of a guy who must have been Gretchen's boyfriend, the one who died before I came to Swan. He looks like Saddam Hussein on a smiley day. Two seats on one side of her desk, her leather throne on the other. There's a couple of filing cabinets and a locked cupboard with glass doors showing bottles and boxes of pills inside. I haven't been in here since she told me that Lolly wasn't going to make it through the night. The radio on the windowsill buzzes classical music. The room gives off a whole *Check me out, I'm brainy and modest—I can totally tell the difference between Bach and Brahms but I'm too cool to brag about it* vibe. She's such a fake.

I'm still standing when Gretchen comes in; she gestures for me to sit. I notice that she's closed the door behind her.

"Listen, Gretchen, I'm expecting a call from my folks, so I really need to get back home. Could we do this some other time? Or you could just send me an email. Whatever."

"Five minutes."

She looks at me with this asshole grin until I finally sit; she fixes her face after that. She has lots of silver hair mixed in with the black. It makes her whole bob shine. There's a beauty mark next to her lips like an old-fashioned movie star, the kind of beauty they don't make anymore, the kind of person I'll never be. God got lazy, or maybe God retired. More likely he got outbid by someone who figured out how to do the whole creation thing cheaper. Now they're just running off copies, sloppy and blurry with generation loss.

"So," she starts, and then leaves a little suspense gap. I force boredom out of my face. *You are the most boring person ever to walk the earth*. "You and Jason looked very smitten yesterday."

Another suspense gap, but it's my turn to fill it.

"Is that a question?"

"I suppose not. I just wanted to make sure that you're"—she leaves another gap, but this one is to tell me that she's about to drop a euphemism—"*taking care* of yourself."

My turn to pause. I feign a shudder. "Sorry, I just threw up in my mouth. Is there, like, a medical term for that?"

"I know the resources on Swan are somewhat limited and I just wanted to make sure you have"—euphemism pause—"*everything you need*."

"I'm all set. Thanks."

She moves to the next thing before I have a chance to get up. She makes my spit hot and bitter as though someplace in my mouth a cut is bleeding hard. "I've noticed you don't go off-island. I don't know all the details of your situation and I don't expect you to tell me, but I feel it's my responsibility to check that everything's"—euphemism pause—"*in order*. Do you have a family doctor on the mainland? Have you ever had a pap smear?"

And I'm up. "Yeah, Gretchen, thanks. That's great. And, yeah, we have a great doctor, so I'm all set. Really. But I have to go. I'm waiting for an important phone call"—the chapel bell rings but it doesn't mean anything—"so I should really take my groceries and get back."

Gretchen gets up too. I think she's going to do something dorky like shake my hand but she just stands there behind her desk, grinning. "If you ever want to talk . . ."

"Yeah, I'll send you a friend request on Facebook."

She shrugs, like *I'm not mad, just disappointed*, walks me to the kitchen, and hands me the paper bag out of the big fridge. I'd be out of here on the quick but there's something I need to say. It feels like I'm waiting for my question to become real so I can say the words, but I know that's pretty much the opposite of how it works. So I just spit it out. "Gretchen, I want to go to the meeting tomorrow. About the Duchess and what you're going to do."

"Didn't Rose speak to you about it?"

"Yeah, she did."

"And what did she say?"

Don't cry. *Do not cry*. "I just thought that you could say something to the others. You know, because I *come* here—almost every day—and she's, you know, we were . . ."

"I'm sure no one would object to you paying your due respects.

Really, no one would deny you that. But we have rules here. We all loved your grandmother and we've been flexible, allowing you to stay with us for the last few months, but I doubt there is anything that can be done in this case."

"I'd just listen. I wouldn't say anything."

"Wouldn't you?" And it's not a question because she half laughs like she's just caught me in a stupid lie, but it was supposed to be a promise. Like I'd try, I'd do my best, if she'd just let me come. But there's no point arguing anyway. I'll probably be gone by tonight.

"Okay, fine." And that's the last thing I say before my throat closes up with helpless anger.

She could thank me. She could say *something*. It's not like I need to come here. Except that I do, I guess. Still, she could, I don't know, acknowledge me, say something to let me know that it matters. What I've been doing for the Duchess matters. On my way down the big front steps I grind my teeth and don't cry at all.

The chapel's empty when I stick my head around the door, so I take a seat in a pew by the entrance and roll a joint. It's a good place to get your feathers smooth. The stone walls and floor are always cool. The air feels more still than it does outside, as though even the oxygen molecules get all respectful and know how to behave in here. I can just sit and break up buds with my fingernails and breathe and let it go. I didn't really think she'd say yes, but I asked. I said it. They need to have their bizarro separatist society and I need to respect that. Or get the fuck out.

The bulletin board says there's a lecture starting soon—*Lesbian Sex, Arthritis, and You*—so I don't linger. Even though I've only been in the chapel for a few minutes, it takes a couple of blinks to get used to the warm and bright of outside. I spark up and make my way back to my little house on a shitty half-assed cliff on the southern tip of Swan.

There's nothing like a joint and a good walk in the fresh air to take the edge off when life feels jagged and frayed. I've tried most drugs, I guess. Not smack, though. If I were curious about it, I'd try it, but I know everything about it already. You know how sometimes you hear old ladies listening to new pregnancy advice, like don't eat stinky cheese or eat prepacked spinach, and they kind of shrug it off and go, "Oh whatever, I smoked a pack a day and slugged half a bottle of sherry for my nerves when I was pregnant with Jimmy and Sally and *they're* fine." The kind of things Mrs. Tyburn would say. Once I heard my mom saying that, except about heroin. She said it to her friend, and I was right there, in the same room with them. She didn't try to whisper or anything. "And look, she's *fine*." I guess she thought it wouldn't matter if I heard since I *was* fine. I *am* fine. I was kind of little then. I don't know, probably ten or eleven. So I've known for a long time that I didn't need to do smack. I always knew how it would be: that I'd love it. I always knew I'd probably find it deeply comforting, like a bed you could bury me in.

I used to drop acid kind of a lot. Mostly on the weekends, but sometimes I'd skip school and drop a couple of tabs or eat some mushrooms. It's a good thing to do when you don't like where you are and you can't do anything about it. And it's good for bridging the gap. When things start getting heavy and girls you know start carrying handbags to school, and people expect you to think about a college major and a career and sex and, like, having a boyfriend you're in love with. By the time you're fourteen or fifteen everyone is trying to be *so* grown up, but tripping lets you get down on all fours if you want, or laugh at something stupid and normal like wallpaper or your reflection in the mirror. You can look at things like you're a baby again. You can play. Maybe not everyone needs to take a break from growing up, but I did.

Some people can't even handle the thought of tripping, but I've always been okay with it. My mom had a talk with me when she found out I was doing acid. She found out the very first time. I was thirteen and by then our rule was that I could pretty much do whatever I wanted but I had to call her and let her know where I was. (They didn't do the same for me; they could disappear for days and I wasn't allowed to say anything. But no one ever told me life was going to be fair.)

So I called her up to say we're all going to a gig and then crashing at my friend Shaggy's, which was completely true, and immediately she goes, "Are you tripping?" Like I wasn't actually talking but singing or moaning or something. And I thought I'd been so cool; I'd practiced what I was going to say standing by the pay phone while the cigarette butts and globs of discarded bubble gum on the sidewalk swam around my feet, before I'd slipped in my quarter and dime and punched my number in.

The next day she sat me down and told me everything I needed to know, laying it down in a firm voice, a whole new set of rules: ice cream to come down, orange juice to trip harder, never talk to cops, avoid hospitals unless your life literally depends on it, and remember that wherever you go, no matter how far away, no matter how fucking weird it gets, you'll always come back. People always come back.

One feeling I used to get all the time was the sense of having no body. It wasn't weightlessness, or some awesome floating or flying thing, or an out-of-body experience. All the normal things you can see on yourself, like the tip of your nose or your feet and maybe your cheeks a little or your hair at the sides, I didn't have any of that. I'd look down and just see the floor.

I had one trip that I really loved. I was convinced that I was a minor character in someone else's dream. The feeling was intensely relaxing. I didn't have to do anything, because everything I did was just a metaphor. And since it wasn't my dream, I didn't have to decode the signs. Nothing made sense but nothing had to. It was the greatest experience I've ever had; for an entire afternoon I didn't have to exist. And I came back.

There's nothing to be afraid of. People come back.

look hard. I blink and strain. Nothing works. I keep trying to say *where, where, where?* but there's no breath in me.

Another landslip while I was gone. Looking at the space where ground used to be is a kick in the chest. My rock is gone. Slipped into the sea without me. By the far corner of the house, the cliff's edge is only three feet or so from the path that wraps around and leads to the back door. At its widest I have maybe six or seven feet of backyard left. My heart's not beating right. It beats lumps and gurgles and it hurts.

Midafternoon. No clouds. I feel exposed. I feel like I'm seconds away from falling.

Wouldn't it be just the worst, like an O. Henry story? My parents finally arrive to bring me back to the mainland and they slip off the side with clumps of dirt and rocks before they can get to the door.

Inside I don't know what to do with myself. I stick the chicken in the fridge. That's the one thing that has to be done. Then there's nothing. The red numbers on the microwave stare at me and I stare back. Lolly set the time five minutes fast. She was like that, efficient even in retirement. I stare and listen for house sounds but there's no noise inside or out. No more explosions. Nothing. There's nothing here. My heart's not beating right.

Up the stairs to Lolly's room. She's not coming back. She's not coming back. I turn the knob and walk across the floor. It doesn't matter that my feet make an impression on the soft gray carpet. She's not here. She's not coming back. She didn't want me but she was all that I had. There are more red eyes in Lolly's room—the DVD player, her TV, her alarm clock. She was into gadgets. Her life was digital. She didn't trust the things I made in the oven and on the stove. When she lived alone she ate at the Psychedelicatessen or heated something up in the microwave. I had to get my head around the difference between her reliance on electronic things and my mother's raw-paleo-whole-foods-clean-eating approach, which Lolly found a clichéd rip-off. Mom didn't think that you could call something that came out of a microwave a meal. Lolly thought of those shortcuts as liberation. She wanted to be efficient and clean, just add water. She bought the appliances that promised to save her time. Time for what? Time to grow old the way she wanted to? When I think about her, I always feel like there wasn't enough time. If I'd had a few more weeks I could have figured out how to be what she needed. She was just too quick for me.

When I got here I tried so hard to make myself useful but Lolly didn't bite. The hard-core separatists aren't subtle. When Lolly and I went out together, they stared and whispered. As if she wasn't aware she was making the Swans bend their rules because her daughter couldn't take care of her own kid. I hated the fact that I'd made her the object of spite. But there was nothing I could do.

It was January, and I was glad to have the excuse to bury my head in a scarf and look down as I walked. The wind picked up specks of sea and froze them and spat them in my face.

I go to her bedside drawer and take out a Valium, pop it on my tongue, and scoop a swallow of water from the tap in her bathroom. A yellow Post-it note reminds me to turn the tap hard so that the water won't drip. I'm so sick of old folks' notes and rules and tuts and kindly advice that I almost ignore it and let it go but my phobia won't let me. I can't stand to think that the water might make its way in here, into my house.

I manage to swallow the next one dry because I can't make myself go back to the faucet and touch the water again. Swallowing takes effort. I have to pull and pull and force spit up into my mouth and try to push it down hard against the pill in my throat. As it tries to stick against the sides, I try to pull up more spit to get it down. Oh God, my heart's not beating right and I have to get this down.

Just in case, I take a third and go through it all again.

My breathing starts to grip onto itself. Lightly. Something gets evened out, those gulping heartbeats start to fall in step with my breaths, and my shoulders drop to what feels like a mile from my ears, and the fear goes out with the tide I can hear outside. I don't like it. I don't like the fact that the waves sound the same as the peace that has started to come over me, but I'm alone and it's better than nothing. This tidal peace is better than nothing.

I tried so hard to make life easier for her. She always saw my parents when she looked at me. I have my father's nose, the shape of his eyes. She never liked to look at him. She said she never understood why they *always* had to do *everything* the hard way.

Why couldn't she see that I was the only other person on earth who knew exactly what she meant?

It changed things for everyone else, too—my being here. I've picked up bits of the story. There had been a meeting before I got here. Lolly briefed the Swans on my situation and they took a vote. The result was not unanimous. But the agreement was that I could stay a while until my parents managed to clean up. She talked about it in terms of days and weeks, let them picture me mostly in my room in Lolly's house, tweeting links to BuzzFeed lists or whatever they think kids do with all their time. I'd leave them alone, and they'd leave me alone.

Three or four days after my parents had gone, I left the house by myself for the first time and ventured into the center. Lolly was off-island doing a day's work at her old company in Portsmouth, and my mind felt like it was eating itself. I'd try to read or watch TV but my attention was pulled out by the tides, up and down, in and out, shifting frequencies that made my skull buzz. At one point I turned everything off and surrendered to existing in the box of my off-blue guest room with the torture music of the Atlantic tide. When I noticed myself laughing, I knew I had to go outside.

The walk to the north side of the island felt longer than it does now. The sky pressed down, threatening snow, and the wind followed me like an asshole bully and I didn't have a pair of gloves. There's something extra terrible about a freezing cold island, like being lost in space. I'd thought for a second that I could make this a useful experience, pleasant even, that this was actually the perfect place to learn how to knit, for example. But then I realized I didn't know who to ask or how. Or, rather, it felt like I couldn't possibly ask anything of anyone. They were already letting me be there, giving me a place to stay so that I didn't have to make the kinds of choices you have to make when you've got nothing and you're alone.

I walked past the chapel. It was silent except for the whirring of the wind like the sound when a CD is about to play on an old machine, so I went up to it and stuck my head around the door. Unfortunately it was tai chi that morning; the Swans do it inside during the winter. They all turned and stared at me like I had a foot growing out of my face. Mostly they smiled. I guess they felt sorry for me.

It's not like it was the first time I'd felt self-conscious, but I'd figured out how to deal with it in the Bad Place. On Swan, I didn't know how to be. Because it's not like when you're shopping and the store detective follows you around the whole time, so you stay there twice as long, and stop and duck under racks and displays, put a pair of sunglasses on your head and make for the exit and then "remember" at the last minute and put them back. You can tease a store detective who gets on your case because you have as much right to be there as anyone. But being seventeen on Swan, I really wasn't supposed to exist; I was a constant reminder of the kind of person the Bad Place prefers—my blank-screen forehead, absence of expression lines, my lack of real knowledge or expertise in anything, really, a stupidity the mainlanders gobble up like baby fat. So I ignored their stares and felt sorry because I was kind of ruining everything. But I thought it would only be a few weeks, a month, two at the most. I only asked Lolly once, and she said they'd be back for me soon. Not as long as this.

By the time I got to Rose's place my toes felt solid and they hurt in this way where I couldn't be sure whether they'd just snapped off. I think I was grimacing when the chimes above her door jingled as I walked in. Rose was up a stepladder stocking a high shelf; she came down, not quickly but lightly, like a strange bird, grabbed my hand, and gave it a massive shake that almost popped my shoulder out of joint. She didn't wait for me to tell her who I was. It's not like I needed to, but I'd always assumed that old people liked formality. Not that one, not Rose. She pointed me toward the freezer where Lolly usually shopped, climbed back up the stepladder, and got back to what she'd been doing. I said maybe my grandmother would like something different, that I was actually pretty good in the kitchen. Rose said *good luck* in kind of a grumble. I picked up some peppers and broccoli, a box of quinoa, and two cans of salmon.

"You better put on more layers, Small-fry."

I found myself grinning. It felt odd. Then I realized that no one had spoken to me for days. Not since my parents left, or when it was Lolly asking me if I needed anything. Mostly she left notes.

Rose went on. "I'll be goddamned if you ain't shaking like a leaf. How 'bout I turn up the fire while you take a seat?" She nodded toward the counter, but when I started to sit on the stool behind it she shouted, "Don't you dare, mad-moi-zelle. You can put yourself up on the counter. Chair's for ol' Rose."

Her back was still turned, but she's the kind of old person who just knows. She has total control of her place, like she and her shop are some kind of team and they talk in a silent, secret language. The red of the heater glowed brighter and started to blow in a louder drone as Rose turned and walked over to me, smoothly so I barely noticed her limp. Then she stopped, her shoulders square with mine, sizing me up. I don't think I gave anything away, but I was sure that whatever she said next would make me cry like the world had come to an end.

"Bet you play a shit hand of poker. Seems to me a kid like you needs to know how to play poker." And just like that she pulled a deck out of her apron pocket and gave me a lesson. A short one, twenty minutes maybe, but she was totally focused, like this was the most important thing she could be doing. And I listened as hard as I could and it was wonderful, not having to think or wonder or worry. Then the bell above the door jingled and Nick walked through. Rose gathered up the cards in a single-handed sweep.

"I think that's enough for today. Why don't you bundle up and scoot on home, get some dinner ready before Violet gets back."

I buttoned my coat, took my bag, and headed for the door.

"Ahem," Rose growled from behind the counter. Nick was staring, as usual. "What d'ya say?"

"Thanks, Rose."

I was almost finished cooking when Lolly came home. It wasn't going to be a masterpiece. She didn't have any real spices—just a jar of some kind of low-calorie, low-sodium flakes—but it was going to be all right.

From the window above the sink I saw Lolly rounding the path to the back door. She had short gray hair, always neat, like a former first lady. The door opened, closed, and then opened again, banging against the wall of the utility room. She sprinted into the kitchen a moment later, fanning her hands and flinging open the windows. I stepped out of the way when she rushed for the stove to turn on the exhaust fan.

"What's burning?"

"Nothing." She looked at me like I was lying, and suddenly it felt like I was. The heat from the oven was gulped up by the open windows and door, and the temperature change was violent. "Just peppers. I was roasting peppers on the flame on the stove. I thought I'd make a sauce to go with the fish cakes I made."

"Oh Jesus, what a mess."

"I was going to clean up when I was done. Are you hungry? It'll be finished in a few minutes."

"No, dear. I had a late lunch." Then she looked away, like she was lying. "I have to finish some reading; I'm back on the mainland tomorrow to finish up this consultancy job. I'll be in my room if you need me. And can you please remember to switch on the fan when you cook? Otherwise smells get everywhere."

"Yeah, sorry about that."

She looked over her shoulder as she left the room. I'd set two places at the table. She looked at me. "No, *I'm* sorry."

The crack man is whistling but he won't pick a tune. He fills the house with the high pitch of the Atlantic wind, the one that drags the waves to my back door. I try to hear something else—house sounds, island sounds—but this thin shriek dominates like a needle through my eardrum, the breeze outside becoming a blade because it shouldn't be here, inside, taking down the walls with the patience of a senior citizen. If I just stay here, mouth shut, in the quiet of my body, which is soft and still from the Valium, maybe they'll just forget about me. Please, please just leave me alone.

My muscles are going soft. The room is spinning slowly. I can't make anything out distinctly. The deep growl of my stomach barks back at the crack man's whistle. I should eat something. Lolly liked a quiet house and I've ruined it.

She never asked me questions. I guess she wanted to keep the peace and quiet she'd built out here. She'd earned it. I wasn't the only one she didn't talk to. She could have chosen a house closer to the center, but she wanted to be out here, away from everyone else's shit. And then I dropped into her lap.

Maybe she didn't ask me questions because she knew everything about me already. And what she didn't know, she could fill in with everything she knew about my mother. Which was unfair, but what was I supposed to do about it? I knew she didn't understand, but she never said anything to me, so I never got the chance to correct her. She just looked at me like I was all wrong, the way you look at a sixth finger or a cat with no tail. Or she didn't look at me. She was really good at not looking at me. When we were alone in the house, time passed like the forming of a scab.

Everything in Lolly's house is digital. Nothing chimes, nothing ticks. Only the phone makes noise, and ever since Lolly died, it doesn't.

Lolly's a clock with no tick and no tock, no pendulum swing, no plastic clack when the minute advances, no second-long flick when the big hand makes its one-degree jump into the next minute, into the future at the exact instant that it becomes the present.

Talk to me, please, talk to me.

I stumble a few times when I try to stand. I can almost see Lolly looking at me, fucked up and underfed, so high on pharmies I can hardly get up off the floor. I see her seeing me and looking away, shaking her head and letting out a sigh. On my feet I'm facing the window. The day outside is too bright and I'm so dizzy with hunger that I can hardly bring myself to go down to the kitchen to cook. The carpet is soft and thick underfoot. It makes me trip so I steady myself on the furniture and against the walls.

My mother says I should stand up straight. She says I'll get a hunchback if I keep walking like this. It's hard but I try to pull my head up, push my shoulders back. She says I'll get depressed if I walk around with my head hidden between my shoulders, that if I walk with more confidence I'll feel more confident. So I try to pull my chin up but I can't do it without crying; still she insists it'll make me feel better.

She says she's proud of me because I know how to take care of myself. She says, "You're so capable. I never have to worry about you, my love."

"That's just your excuse to fucking ignore me!"

But when I scream back at her she's gone and the house almost shakes with the sickening quiet, and my head drops down again and I want to fall onto the living-room floor until I hear her whisper, "Posture," gently, in that singsong way she uses when she knows what she's saying is a pain in the ass but she has to say it anyway.

"I know, I know." I think I'm standing up straight.

I put the chicken on a board.

"Don't you dare start before you preheat the oven."

Three hundred fifty degrees. Mom fake-frowns at my impatience, so I lower it to 325. I like the click when the oven light switches on; I like the sound the fan makes. The air feels less empty; I lean my head back and listen.

Then Lolly's there and she claps her hands at me. She's right—I'm not paying attention to what I'm doing. This is how accidents happen. This is how absentminded little girls accidentally burn the house down.

"Leave her alone, Mom. She knows what she's doing. My girl has always been so capable."

I don't know whose side to take, so I leave them to bicker and turn on the exhaust fan and open the windows because I know that Lolly hates it when I fill her house with cooking smells.

The horn from the afternoon boat blows in. The three of them could be coming back, all three could be back here in another twenty minutes, and I'll have dinner in the oven and Mom will be proud because she's the one who taught me about tarragon and Lolly will be happy that I remembered to open the windows and turn on the fan and my dad will do that thing he does where he says that the food needs something, so he has to keep tasting it, because he's still not sure and he just keeps taking bites with this fake-confused look on his face until he's eaten his entire plate of food, because no matter how cool you used to be, once you become a dad you automatically develop some dorky, embarrassing spiel that's so cute that no one can tell you to fuck off and stop being so goddamn goofy.

"You wouldn't talk to your father like that anyway, would you?"

That has to be Lolly, the way everything she says is a question and an assumption and an instruction, but her voice is a lot like my mother's and I wonder if it's also a lot like mine, so I say, "Which one of you does my voice sound like? When I talk, when I say things out loud, does my voice sound like yours? Or yours?"

"It's like mine. You take after me exactly."

"No, I think she's equally dissimilar from both of us."

And they start to argue again, not looking at me but facing each other, and I try to listen to the fan noises and the seagulls screaming and barking on the rocks outside. I touch my knee to the oven door and the heat makes their voices quieter, so I hold it there until my body yanks itself away from the hurt and I pant a little and my mother turns to me again and says, "Daydreaming over a hot oven. That girl of mine, so capable but she never pays enough attention."

Then Lolly adds, "Children need structure," and they're at it again, and I'm still panting and I think I'm weirdly smiling, and I place the chicken on the cutting board on the counter, pull the left leg outward with my left hand, and strike down at the hip joint with my right.

I hear my mother say, "You'll never get through it if you act like you're doing a playground hand-clap game. Again. With intention this time."

I nod at her and try again, really pushing with my shoulder with proper follow-through. This time the leg pops out of joint properly. I wiggle it, push the bone up, and run my finger over the ball at the end of the socket. It's pearly and satisfyingly smooth. Before my mother can get on my case for spacing out again, I turn the chicken around and do the other leg. I can feel my mother smiling. She's here; she's on her way.

I tuck some tarragon inside the cavity, under the breast skin, inside the legs and wings, take my length of dental floss and start to truss the chicken. Under the bishop's nose, looping around the ankles, pulling the legs tight, elevating the breast, then around the sides, past the thighs, tying it in a square knot under the neck.

"See, Mom? See what she can do?"

"Great, Bella. Now maybe your child can get a job in a chicken-trussing factory. That's really some future you've given her."

I put it in a roasting pan and put the pan in the oven while my mother's and grandmother's voices get louder and louder, their blaming and cheap shots turning into gibberish. When I look at them they're a blur, their voices become pressure like each one is stamping on one of my temples, trying to hurt each other through my body. And I press my hands against my ears but it doesn't keep the noise out and doesn't make the pain stop and I'm so dizzy I could throw up, so I try to stop the spinning by fixing my eyes on something static in front of me, reaching out to grab something still to keep my body and my brain from spinning anymore and puking out the nothing that's burning a hole in my stomach, and the first thing, the closest thing, is the heavy wooden knife block. I steady myself on it with both hands, and then pull the chef's knife out of its slot.

It's the kind of thing you have to do in one breath. Hard, like you mean it. With intention. The heel of the knife cracks through my jeans and half an inch or so into my thigh, and soon blood pours out, thick and generous. The ghosts of my mother and grandmother are quiet. I hear the waves roar at the rocks outside. I wail back at the waves. I hear them again when I breathe in and wail back louder. My face streams salt water and I scream and shake and it almost feels like the sea and me are evenly matched.

I'm on the floor somehow. So's the knife. If you don't look after knives properly they go dull. You shouldn't leave them lying around. I can't just leave knives lying around like this. I pull myself up. It's hard, though. I don't want to get up. I have to wipe my eyes a few times. I reach down and pick up the knife. My jeans are all stained on the right side. I wonder for a second if I'm still bleeding. Not that I care, really. I'm just curious.

It's hard to turn on the faucet to wash the knife. It's another one-breath job. Even with rubber gloves on it's too much for me right now, and the crying starts all over again. It's not so bad this time, probably because I'm crying over something real—the pain in my throbbing leg.

I dry the knife and put it back into the block, and then slide down, pressing my back against the cabinets on my way back to the floor. It's like someone rubbing my back. Almost. And the thought is so pathetic that before I know it I'm streaming again.

———

My mother's underwater. She's drowning. She's screaming because she's drowning. I must be underwater too because I can hear her. But it's dark. I turn around and around and the water is the noise and I can't breathe.

And then, for just a second, it isn't water or screaming. It's the phone. I scramble onto my feet and lunge for the receiver. It's hard to speak at first but I force two "hellos" down into the mouthpiece. I don't understand the noise that comes back. And then I realize it's the dial tone. It's not my mother—it's not even the phone. The oven timer. Dinner's ready. I take the food-formerly-known-as-Calvin out of the oven and I burn my thumb on the pan. The pain is that strange, nearly numb pain, an un-hurt. I mean, the hurt makes me feel a little better, more awake, less worried. I start to feel a sense of where I am, what time it is. The clock on the microwave says 7:15. The last boat has come and gone. I cover the chicken with foil to let the meat rest for twenty minutes. How am I going to eat all this food before it goes bad?

What a shame.

Twenty minutes to kill.

I should feel lucky. Mrs. Tyburn gave me a job that almost pays the bills and other than that I don't have anywhere I have to be. I can choose the way I spend my days off. I can be alone whenever I want. I have a place to sleep. I have food. I have Rose. But someday soon I'll have to go.

My leg throbs. I'm going to have to throw these jeans out. But the bleeding stopped while I was passed out on the kitchen floor. Things could be worse.

The last boat to Appledore has come and gone and no one came for me. I could turn on the TV and pretend I'm not alone, curl up and try to keep my mind blank until I manage to sleep. But that's hours away. And even though I feel like toxic waste, I want to go out. Rose never invites me; I don't want to miss it. If I'm going to go to the tavern, I have to get my shit together. No one's going to come along and rub my back and say, *There, there, poor baby*. Not today.

The Valium fug is wearing off and I'm getting a grip on my body again. The sunset cuts in through the open windows in reds and oranges. I open and close my hands in this weird, compulsive way, and it's almost like I'm a boxer. There's a determined bounce in my walk as I pace the few clutter-free patches of living-room floor and make my way upstairs. The sea could come pounding in and I'd be able to fight it off. Nick can "accidentally" switch on the sprinklers while I'm working in the garden on a chilly afternoon, and sneer and stare to keep me out of the tavern and the chapel, but this is my house. It may be your island, and I might be forty-eight years off the basic entry requirement, but this house is *mine*. I carry the debt and no one can make me leave until I'm good and ready.

Even with the big, internal pep talk, I hesitate at Lolly's door, hugging my laptop to my chest like a shivering waif peering into a bakery window. If I keep playing the waif, though, I'll never get anywhere. I catch myself, leave the starving kid on the cobble-stones, and go in to get what I need. I put on a CD—one of Lolly's, some French guy called Jacques Brel—and look for something to wear.

Rose told me to meet her at sundown, which is any minute now. Fashionably late—that's what I'll say if she's mad. I settle on a dress, knee-length and brown with white and yellow flowers. I actually look okay, a throwback to that granny look from the nineties. Once I'm dressed I almost leave the closet door open, just to be bad, but can't quite let myself. I take the stupid Post-it off, though, and flush it down the toilet along with the Post-it from the bathroom that says not to put anything in the toilet other than "what it was built for." So there.

Even though I'm probably already late, two more minutes to check my email won't hurt. Spam, circulars, nothing in my inbox that actually has my name on it. Bank balance hovering stubbornly at the *not enough* level. I decide to take a quick peek at the back end of Nick's operating system, and I delete the script that's been making his browser blurry. It was an infantile trick anyway. Then I check his online banking. He's not getting off the hook entirely. One of his monthly direct debits is a donation to the Christian Children's Fund, so I make a duplicate payment to go out next week. Into my Bitcoin wallet, of course—I wouldn't be stupid enough to use my cash account. The bank will cover the mistake, so it isn't really stealing, not from anyone but the bank. And it's pretty much their fault the kids are poor in the first place. It'll get me where I'm going—once I figure out where that is. If I need any more, I've got all his keystrokes. By the time he notices, I'll be long gone.

I shove a few dollars, some pot, and my cell phone into one of Lolly's square, brown handbags. As it goes in, I check my phone—no missed calls. It makes me wonder if my parents still have this number. If I leave and they don't have it, they'll call the house phone. And if I'm not here . . .

I go to the living room to change the outgoing message on Lolly's answering machine. I hit record and after a couple of embarrassing false starts I get something down: *You have reached* (do I say my name? Lolly's?) Erase. *Violet Sadler cannot take your call right now* (yeah, that's a fucking understatement . . .) Erase. Breathe. This isn't rocket science. *We cannot take your call, but please leave a message or, if your message is urgent, please call* (pause—it'll take them a second to find a pen) *603-555-4966. That's six-oh-three, five-five-five, four-nine-six-six. Again, 603-555-4966.*

To double-check, I dial the landline from my cell. Hearing the ring startles a little scream out of me. It's painful to hear, like a crying baby that I can't pick up. Six rings, then there's a click and the message plays. After the beep I say, *Testing, just a test to check that this piece-of-shit twentieth-century technology is still operational* . . . I can see the tape rolling, taking it down.

The path around the house is narrow, and I press myself against the outside wall to keep as far as possible from the edge. It feels like I'm sneaking out, which helps, I think. I'm excited. I am.

It's getting dark. The water on my left shows residue of the whole brilliant sunset thing. On my right the ocean reminds me of some sleazy guy's hair, super-black and shiny at the tips with a slick, sweeping texture and a general not-quite-right-ness. Or a huge bucket of eels and leeches—slimy, sucking, biting monsters.

The sky and the sea are twins, outsized, uninhabitable, changing all the time with the light. The sky plays nice, mostly, aloof and distant. The sea's the dangerous one.

I know it's everybody's dream to live by the water, but water's horrible if you think about it. Like floods—whenever there are floods the sandbags piled up against the door don't quite do the trick, and floodwater gets in, and somehow floodwater's always contaminated with sewage and malaria and shit like that. So it gets through the sand (the sand must be in on it, a scheming old friend) and soaks into everything and starts to rot out your life from the inside. And pretty soon you're up on the roof trying to attract a rescue. But the place you get rescued to is worse than the rotting place you left because people who've lost everything have a tendency to go crazy, and too many crazy people in one place is a war.

Bang. Bang. The wind brings new blasts grumbling up from Duck. Even the ground has turned against me now.

The lights coming from the first houses I encounter are comforting. I could really torture myself thinking about all these future scenarios. It's fucked. But I don't have to live in the future. When I can switch off my doom predictor, the present is actually okay. It's a warm night with the noise of bugs in the grasses giving the air a nice texture. The water is still a couple of paces away from my door. And I'm an adult. Everything is under control.

I almost walk right past the chapel, but turn back and decide to ring the bell.

Ooo. Giddy and Milton are making out in one of the back pews.

"Don't mind me," I singsong at them when they look up, faces flushed candy pink and plum brown.

"Hi, hey. Hey, kid," Giddy sputters. Milton whispers something in Giddy's ear and she snorts a laugh as they get up to leave.

I walk down the stone aisle and into the room where a gnarled, thick rope hangs in the center. It's satisfyingly stuffy and old-smelling in here. I tug and the bell sways. The hammer's dangling like a uvula and then it knocks against the side of the bell. Iron strikes metal with wince-making harshness that softens almost instantly and radiates out in all directions and envelops me. I ring it eighteen times, but I'm sure no one's counting.

CHAPTER ELEVEN

The night is lacy around me. In the east the brighter stars are starting to poke through the inky blue. There are three in a row that I've always thought were Orion's belt. I'm not sure if someone told me that or if I made it up. It reminds me of the Underground Railroad and all the escaped slaves making their way north, the way I'm going now. They read the stars like a map. I wouldn't have been able to do that. I would have been lost, and then discovered, tracked down, and dragged back to be made an example of. There's one star that's really big and bright; it's either Venus or the International Space Station.

Clouds are passing fast. Smaller ones meet and blob together. Their shadows play across the water as it creeps out forever to the east. One cloud is so fat and wet and swollen it looks like it's about to puke. It slinks and flops over the moon with odd wispy tendrils dangling under it like a jellyfish.

Going up to the Relic is a bit like walking into Lolly's bedroom. I shouldn't be here. I should wait for Rose outside. If I try to go in without her, I might just get thrown out right away.

But then I'm just standing there at the bottom of the stairs staring up with my sad waif eyes. Helen and Nancy walk by and wave, but they keep looking back at me. I turn to walk up the wheelchair ramp, except my first step on it makes loads of noise, not that anyone's listening, but it makes me feel self-conscious, so I take the stairs and pause again at the door. Maybe Rose is waiting for me inside. I mean, she did say to meet her at sunset, so I'm late, and why would she just be standing outside somewhere in the dark with the bugs biting when she could have gone inside? There's a big brass thing in the center of the double doors shaped like a steering wheel—a boat one, not a car one. I'm not sure what to do with it. It doesn't seem like I should turn it. And then I notice Lyall looking at me through the window. He raises his pencil-sharp eyebrows, and after maintaining a longish and pretty brutal stare he mouths *pull*. So the steering wheel thing is actually two decorative handles that part in the middle. Great; I'm the champion of the flawless first impression.

The tavern is cool inside. Temperature-wise. Decor-wise, not so much. Fishing nets hang from a couple of the corners and over the bar, with plastic seaweed and fish stuck in them. I get that they're going for irony, a self-aware kitsch, but come on. The fake treasure chest at the end of the bar, in front of the painting of mermaids with huge boobs basking on a rock, is, in my humble opinion, a little too tacky. But I like the dark wood of the bar and the green velvet on the chairs and stools.

I lean against the bar, casual as hell, but behind my back I'm gripping it like I'm afraid gravity's about to fail. I scan the booths. It's much roomier in here than it looks from the outside. The blond Swans are sitting in a booth near the entrance with a bottle in an ice bucket. I wonder if the three of them ever do anything on their own. But it must be nice, having a little group. It must feel like always knowing where you are. They're all really beautiful. I wonder if that's a condition for entry to their clique.

Frances and Ernie are sitting together, both reading books. Ernie's smoking a pipe. It smells like Christmas, which I guess is why they let him get away with smoking inside. Oh God, Gretchen will probably be here. I know she won't tell Rose what a bitch I was this afternoon but I should say sorry anyway. Keep the peace.

The blond Swans have stopped talking. I try to turn my body away from them and angle my head so I can look at them without looking like I'm looking at them. I need to see if they're looking at me, if they've gone quiet because they're whispering about me— wondering if they should say something, wondering what I'm doing here, and what I'm still doing here. But I'm not doing anything. I haven't done anything wrong. Rose invited me. It's not my fault.

Shit, Frances looks up from her book and catches my eye. She waves, elbows Ernie, and he waves too. They're smiling and they almost look like they want me to come over, but that must be wishful thinking, and in a few seconds they're looking back down at their books. I just want to be somewhere on earth where I'm not seconds away from getting kicked out or moved on or beaten up or pushed around until I give up and slink away.

Behind me someone clears their throat. It's Lyall. I turn to find a silent question in his single lifted eyebrow and pursed lips.

I've never actually been introduced to Lyall. He mostly sleeps during the day and spends his nights running the tavern. I've spotted him carrying a crate of lemons from Rose's shop to the Relic, or just leaving the Psychedelicatessen as I cross the grass on my way in.

Seeing him up close catches me off guard. He has a mustache that starts blond in the middle, just under his nose, and then gets gradually darker going along either side into a curl with a point at the end. The spike of black hair under his bottom lip is framed by a sharp goatee that makes the bottom of his face look like an old-timey weapon. When he blinks I can see a thick layer of black glitter covering his eyelids. Big, tree-branch smile lines next to his eyes spread out until the thin tips of all the lines reach his temples. He wears a big gold hoop in his right ear. His slick black hair is pulled into a skinny ponytail on the top of his head. His T-shirt says "Pirates Do It Better."

Oh God, I have to say something to him. Rose, where are you? "Hi. You're Lyall. Sorry."

"Sorry?"

"Right. Um, I'm, um. I'm Violet's granddaughter."

"No!"

"Yeah. You knew that. Sorry."

"As a matter of fact, I did. Now, my little scamp, before you say another word I just want to make one thing absolutely clear. Are you?"

"Am I what?"

"*Are* you or *aren't* you?"

Oh, for Christ's sake, where the fuck is Rose?

Lyall angles his body back and grips the bar with his fingertips. His mouth hangs open in bitchy mock-shock. "Oh. My. God. You *are*. Well, listen here, Gidget. I'm not buying any fucking Girl

Scout cookies, not one box, if you're out of Samoas. You're not going to offload all your wretched, boring, fattening shortbread things on me. And if I may offer some advice, you'd get a hell of a lot more business peddling your factory-baked cellulite-inducers if you wore your uniform."

What the fuck's a gidget?

"Fine! *One* box of Thin Mints. Hear me? One. Payment on delivery. Never pay for anything in advance. A little piece of advice from me to you, free of charge."

"Wow. Thanks."

"Fill in your little order form or whatever. I have customers. 'Scuse me."

Lyall flicks his ponytail at me as he goes to the end of the bar. Great. Nick and Jack are here. When Nick spots me he's so surprised that it takes him a sec to put on his casual hate face. Lyall brings them two beers and the three of them stand there talking. I keep finding myself looking over to see if Nick is trying to stare me out of the room. He does look up once in a while. I try to look away but he catches me every time.

Maybe I should leave. But I just stand there, shifting my weight in a futile attempt to stay still, trying to read anything I can make out from the place where I'm stuck at the far end of the bar. I can just about read the place-names on a map of the Shoals on the opposite wall. I read all the labels on the booze bottles, a fake WANTED poster, some of the postcards behind the big brass and green cash register.

My stomach's churning, all hot with acid, when the door swings open. Rose has her hair teased up high. She's wearing a floor-length, rust-colored halter dress—the kind of thing where if you found it in someone's attic you'd be fucking stoked. She's busy thumbing a text into her phone, but when she looks up she sees me right away and rushes over. She gives me a big look up and down. She's just being nice, obviously, but it's sweet of her.

"Is that Violet's dress?" She doesn't wait for me to answer before she adds, "Looks like it's yers now; suits you down to the ground," and smacks a big *mwah* kiss on what feels like my entire cheek. Then she bounces her fist on the bar. "Lyall! Stop yer slackin'! We're gonna give our girl her first champagne."

Lyall leaves Nick and Jack and saunters up to us real slow, pushing his hips out like a supermodel, making fun of Rose's impatience. I catch the look that passes between them and realize they're flirting. Then he shoots a stern face at me. "*Identification?*"

"What, this one? She's old as hell! Eighteen today!"

"The authorities inform me that the drinking age is twenty-one in New Hampshire."

"And the age to live on Swan is sixty-five—in case no one mentioned that to you . . ." That's Nick, being helpful.

Lyall looks at Nick and then frowns a long frown at Rose. He turns his back to us, and when he turns back I'm too busy examining his sharp, made-up face to notice what he's doing until I hear the thump thump thump of him setting three shot glasses down on the bar.

"We've exhausted our supply of champagne, I'm afraid." He pours three shots of tequila and pulls out a saltshaker and three fat wedges of lime.

"Guess we'll have to make do, eh, Small-fry?" Rose licks her hand and shakes on some salt. Lyall goes next, then me.

"Happy Birthday, cutie."

My chest is warm and I feel myself smiling.

"Beer back?" Lyall asks.

"You know it!"

Lyall brings us two Mexican beers with foil around the necks. Some's dangling on the lips of mine and I pick it off so I don't get that horrible foil-on-your-teeth thing before I take a pull. We lean against the bar; a drum kit and mics and shit are set up on the little stage at the end. "Blue Monday" by New Order is finishing and that Arctic Monkeys song starts up after it.

Rose elbows me in the side. "You wanna dance, don't cha, junior?"

I didn't realize it but I guess I'd been moving. "Are you offering?"

"Not me, not tonight, no, ma'am. Hip's acting up—rain on the way."

It's cool how she can tell the weather by her body.

"Lyall, this new door policy of yours—didn't see fit to put it to a vote?"

Lyall looks at me; he clearly knows what Nick means. Fucker. I should have left his screen just the way it was, make him go back to the Bad Place and buy a whole new computer. But Lyall raises his eyebrows and says to him, "Please don't tell me you plan to start coming here in white sneakers. That I simply can't abide. On you, that is. Proper shoes make you look so much more distinguished."

"It's not the dress code that's bothering me. It's the company.

Seems you'll let anybody in nowadays. Better watch those standards. Slipping, slipping. Too many slips and the whole house falls down . . ." He's looking right at me; he's not even trying to hide it.

"*Ignore* him," Rose murmurs into my shoulder. And that's what I'm going to do. I'm going to ignore him. I put on a smile and laugh at nothing. I fight with the niggling urge to see if he's still staring at me. But I don't look. I do as Rose tells me and keep my attention on drinking my beer.

Then it occurs to me that it's impossible to ignore someone. It's necessarily a contradiction because when you're ignoring someone you're paying them this special, unique kind of attention, like they're actually the most important person in the world. You're doing this odd performance just for them, paying more attention to someone you hate than you would to someone you love. Maybe to ignore someone really means failing to drop dead no matter how much they want you to. If that's the game between me and Nick, I'm totally winning.

The door opens and Earl has barely stepped into the tavern before Rose is squealing. "Git on in here, ya sonofabitch, and git a round in!"

"What's the occasion?"

Lyall flings his arms out. "The natal day of our young guest. Joy to the world."

"Small-fry here's eighteen today," Rose adds.

"Well, well. Lyall, I suppose we'll have to get this young person her first champagne."

"Fresh out," Rose and Lyall say together.

"Okay, then that'll be another round for the ladies. And for me . . . When did you last clean your lines, Lyall?"

"Earl, darling, my pipes are clean."

"Proof of the pudding's in the eating, I guess. Right, pint of IPA, easy on the head."

Lyall starts to come back to that but closes his mouth so his lips make an audible slap. "No, not in front of the kid, I think. You're lucky you keep gentle company, darling."

It's not until Lyall's poured half of Earl's beer that Earl's face shows he's got the joke. He laughs a little *heh heh heh* laugh and wags a finger at Lyall. Lyall smiles and blows him a kiss.

As the three of us settle down at a table, I suddenly have to pee so bad my teeth itch.

Rose's eyes drop down to my knee, which is bouncing at the speed of machine gun fire. "Now, if y'all'll excuse us, we're gonna have a gossip and gussy-up." She takes my hand and we walk to the bathroom like girlfriends.

Peeing is the most wonderful thing in the world. It is total, full-body joy. Whoever was in here before me had asparagus. I don't know why, but smelling someone else's asparagus pee always turns me on a little. God, I am a weird fucking pervert. And I hate having thoughts like these around other people, because once you think the thought consciously, really registering it, there's always the danger that in two more drinks' time you'll be blathering your dorkiest secrets to everyone.

Rose is waiting for me by the sink, poufing up her hair in the back. The skin around her cleavage is deeply wrinkled and soft-looking. I don't stare. She takes a tube of lip gloss out of her bag, puts some on, and offers it to me as she presses her lips together and pouts and scrapes the excess away from the edges of her lips with her orangey-pink fingernails. I memorize the steps and mimic her. She checks her phone.

"I sure hope Giddy didn't take a spill or nothin'. Said she'd meet us an hour ago, and now she's not returnin' my SMS messages. You think we should call in?"

"Maybe we should give it another hour." I lean in, just in case someone comes in and overhears. And because it's nice to be close to Rose. "She might be, um, busy. I caught her making out with Milty in the chapel earlier . . ."

"No! When?"

"On my way here."

"Ooo, and they're still at it?"

"They left while I was ringing the bell."

Rose takes out her phone and thumbs in a text as we head back to the table. She shows it to me before she hits send: *Bad gurlz make the baby jesus cry.*

Hazel comes over with a tray of tequila shots and a bowl of limes. I wash down the scratchy, burning taste with a long swig of my second beer but make a point to pace myself after that.

"So, another year closer to the good life, eh? Shame about all the shit in the middle . . ." Hazel says.

Rose swipes the air at her. "Oh, you hush, now."

But Hazel swallows a leftover shot, gnashes through a lime wedge, and carries on: "Taxes, traffic, cheating spouses"—Hazel's had three husbands—"kids that talk back, arthritis, menopause, cancer . . ."

Hazel, Rose, and Earl pick up their glasses, tap them against the tabletop, raise them again, and take a long drink.

". . . caesarean scars, stretch marks . . ."

"*I* have stretch marks," I say.

"Aw, go on," Rose says, "you *do not*."

"I do. I've had them since I was thirteen and my ass happened."

This cracks everybody up. Across the table and over the roaring Wrinklies, Hazel shouts at me, "Kid, ever tried a Dark and Stormy?"

Without waiting for me to answer, she passes me her pale yellow drink.

"Easy now," Rose sings. "Beer before liquor . . ."

It's sweet and cold, which is nice at this moment. It's starting to get hot in here.

Trumpets blare in a show-offish way from a swing-punk track—maybe Voodoo Glow Skulls or the Bosstones or something.

"Come on, kiddo. Let's cut a rug." Earl holds out a hand to me and pulls me out to the center of the floor.

And because it's Earl he has to teach me the jitterbug before we can really start dancing. Back-step, right, left-right-left. Back-step, right, left-right-left. But the music is too fast for me to count along and also know which foot is which, so I'm basically jogging around as he pretty much just bounces on the spot, and I'm spinning and spinning and can barely hold myself up from twirling and laughing. The next song is a slower one, a lady crooner singing a poppy list of nice things in Portuguese. Now I actually do have to pay attention to my feet, which always seem to go the opposite way from the way I'm telling them to go, but then I realize it's because I'm watching Earl's feet, which I keep stepping on. And every time I do he makes a comedy yowl like he's just been shot with an arrow by a cartoon "Indian."

And then Paul Simon comes on. "I'm going to sit this one out."

"You dance divinely, my dear," Earl mews in a fake English accent and kisses me on the cheek.

Back at the table, Rose leans in for a secret. "Giddy's not gonna make it, but she says give you a kiss from her and Milty. I reckon that Jezebel done got into her grandson's stash of the bitty blue boys, so they might not be surfacing for some time."

Ew.

And then I remember something Lyall said before. "Hey, Rose, what's a gidget?"

She throws her head back and slaps the table. "Listen to this, y'all. Small-fry here saying to me, 'Rose, what's *a Gidget*?'!"

And all the Wrinklies are laughing again, but more *at* me this time. Fine, no one's going to tell me. I'll Google it when I get home. So when I get a tap on the shoulder I'm happy to see someone *not* in a hilarity spasm, even though it's Gretchen.

"Why didn't you tell me it's your birthday?"

I shrug. Sorry to be a bitch, but what a stupid question.

"Anyway, I brought you this. Doctor's orders: reading a book with an actual plot might do you good."

Moby Dick, title embossed into the leather cover. I flip through and every now and then there's a ye olde sketch of whale anatomy or a harpoon or something. I half want to give her a hug, and I totally owe her one. So I get up and do it. "Sorry for being a brat today."

She squeezes my shoulders. "Let me know what you think."

Ted leans in to see what I got and tells me a little bit about it 'cause apparently it's his favorite book. The old-timey cash register dings whenever anyone pays for a drink, which isn't actually that often because most of the Wrinklies put stuff on their tab and settle up with Lyall later on, but it's enough to keep a ringing in the air. My mother would love it. My father would probably echo the dings and would keep doing it long after it became annoying. And my mother would know how to ignore him and have a good time anyway. They'd like it here. They should have come.

Drinks keep appearing in front of me. I tune in and out of conversations. The people in them keep changing. Chairs scrape the wooden floor as new Swans pull up seats to join our table or leave it to join others. Helen cuddles up on Nancy's lap to free up a seat when Marie arrives in black and purple velvet and lace, clanking with jewelry. The blondes are staring into the middle of their table at one of their phones. The look on their tilted faces says they're looking at pics of someone's grandkids.

"This world, I'll tell you what . . ."

"Ain't what it used to be . . ."

"Going straight to hell."

God, it's hot in here.

The place is mostly full when Suzie Q and Johnny Come Lately crash in like cops on a drug bust, Suzie with her bass and Johnny with his guitar strapped across his back, his amp in one hand and a bottle of whiskey in the other. Everything about the room turns up—everyone starts laughing a bit louder, the cash register dings more often, the Swans move between the tables more. Bottles sometimes drop and sometimes break. It's Saturday.

Suzie and Johnny march through the bar giving little bits of attention to everyone, and the Wrinklies eat it up like candy. Johnny makes for the bar and kisses Lyall on the mouth before moving up to the stage, giving everyone a different wave or kiss or secret handshake along the way. Suzie's shtick is similar but she takes a different route, does more talking and dancing, takes more time working the room. Neither of them say anything to me. Which is really fucked up. I mean, you can never tell if people even give a tiny bit of a shit about you. I thought we were friends. Not super-tight like me and Rose or the Duchess, but still. Maybe they only tolerate me because of Jason.

By the time Suzie reaches the stage, Johnny's negotiated various wires and cables and is tapping the microphone and tuning his guitar. She takes her bass out of its case and starts doing the same while Frances takes a seat behind the drums.

I reach for my beer bottle but it's empty, so I take the one next to it, *accidentally*, 'cause I don't think anyone's looking anyway . . .

And, like, where is Jason? This is nice; he should be here. I think about calling him, but maybe it would be better to send him a dirty text, or a picture with my top off. No, that's hideous. I'm not twelve.

Frances taps the drums and the noise in the bar reduces to a grumbly hum with chairs scraping the floor as people move to see better.

Suzie Q puts her mouth to the microphone. "Looks like unuther mighty fine Saturday on the magic Isle of Swan. I seen Wrinklies here reach their eighth and ninth decades between these creaky ol' walls, but this'll be a first for me, celebrating a squeaky-green eighteen! Kiddo, fer yer birthday, Johnny and me, well, we didn't git you nothin'. But my ol' man here says you might be fond of this."

And I can't believe what comes next. They play *Workingman's Dead*, my favorite Grateful Dead album, right through, doing all the Garcia and Hunter melodies. The tickle of the first notes of "Uncle John's Band" makes me cry a little. Then Rose and I sway and sing along to "High Time." Grover buys me a bourbon. "A proper American drink with proper American music," he says. And somehow I find myself on stage sharing Suzie Q's microphone, singing the chorus to "Dire Wolf." Because it's so good, and they're all coaxing me, and how can you resist when the time comes, and you've had some beers, how can you not get up and belt your best?

This is the best party I've ever been to. Nick must have fucked off home, and it feels sublime being here. I've never been popular before, and tonight it's easy to pretend I really am.

Peeing again. Peeing. Is. Excellent. It's the only thing that involves water that actually feels good. It even sounds good, when the stream hits the side, and you can push it out really hard, and when you've been drinking it goes on forever, which is wonderful.

Except Jason isn't at the party. He should be here. Everybody loves Jason and Jason loves me. Maybe I'll send him a text, except my phone isn't in my pocket. I look around and I can't find it, even though it's suddenly really bright and I'm all alone.

Then someone knocks on the door. I'm still in the bathroom.

Great. Now I need to puke. If I breathe hard I'll be able to get some fresh air into my stomach and that'll calm things down. But I have to leave because someone else needs to get in here.

I don't have to puke. I'm fine.

My phone's on the table. No missed calls, no messages. But it's fine because all of my friends are here. Except . . . where's Rose? I can't see her. I get up and look around the bar. I can't make out anyone's face very well. Just shapes, like we've all broken up into symbols. I take a sip of beer to unstick my tongue from the roof of my mouth.

I'm standing up. What was I doing? Oh, yeah, looking for Rose. She doesn't smoke, but maybe she's outside getting some air. It's really hot. I'm trying to figure out my feet, how I'll step between the chairs and people without stepping on anyone or knocking anything over or falling down. But Helen and Nancy sidle up on each side of me.

"Did all your birthday wishes come true?" Helen whisper-shouts into my ear.

"Everything!" It's the lie she wants to hear. The lie I want to tell. So it's almost the truth.

"Beautiful baby," Nancy coos and kisses my cheek.

I love them. I love this night.

I've lost Rose. She wouldn't have just left without saying anything. She wouldn't have just left me. Maybe she's in the bathroom doing a line with someone. God, I'm really tired. The skin on Nancy's hands falls, makes valleys between the knuckles and bones as she rolls a massive joint. She spreads her fingers wide, curling the edge of the paper over the leaves, and rolls the whole thing up tight and tidy.

The band wraps up with "Casey Jones." The pitch of the whistles and wails from the Wrinklies makes me wince. Nancy gestures with her eyebrows and we go outside with our sword-length doobie.

"You got greens, birthday girl."

I spark it up. Her hash is chocolatey and warm. The joint and the cool air on my face and arms calm my stomach, but looking up at the sky is a mistake. The gaps in the black clouds are full of too many stars. It's too big; it's all too much. Where am I? Where's Rose? My mouth feels glued shut. I have nothing to say to Nancy. I feel for the steps and sit down, a little embarrassed at how fucked up I've gotten.

Reading my mind, Nancy reaches into her bag and hands me a bottle of water. I love old people. They fucking know *everything*.

"Where should I go, Nan? You've been everywhere." My words aren't coming out clearly. I can hear my tongue in my mouth when I talk. "Should I go to Europe?"

I pass the joint, which is awkward since it's pretty much as long as my forearm. Nancy takes a draw. Thinking lines settle across her face. "Europe's spent, kid. Maybe the Balkans, though . . ."

That makes me laugh. "I don't know where that is. What about California?"

"California's going to fall into the ocean. San Fran's gone the way of Woodstock."

I've been to Woodstock. It's pretty silly. Lots of middle-aged people in designer hippie gear. "Fine, then, I'll go to Tibet and hang out with the Dalai Lama."

"Dalai Lama's gone, kid. Don't they teach you anything in school?"

"I don't go to school."

"I guess that's why you need to travel."

"Exactly."

I don't want any more of the joint, and Nancy doesn't pass it back, so I must look as wasted as I feel. I finish the whole bottle of water. I don't think she minds.

"The question you're asking me doesn't have an answer, kid. You're not going to find the good spots in any of the guidebooks or websites. You've gotta keep going until somewhere feels right. Trial and error. Lots of it. Trial and error." She puts out the joint on a rock and hands it to me. "Don't smoke it all at once."

She goes in but I stay, sitting on the tavern steps, taking in the stars and the night sounds and even the fear of how big the sky is and how long life is going to be.

When I finally spot Rose she's cuddled up in a booth by the stage sucking face with Suzie Q. I walk in and perch at the bar.

Johnny rocks up and knocks his hip against mine. "Come here often?"

"No"—I'm feeling kind of frisky now—"it's my first time."

"Lyall! Two brews, my man."

Johnny and I clink our bottles and turn and lean our backs against the bar, checking out who's still here. The blondes have gone. Frances looks keyed up, talking to Gretchen as much with her hands as with her voice. Gretchen is listening with a serious face on. Grover and Ernie are talking. One is explaining something to the other but it's hard to tell who's doing which. Lyall balances a curved tower of glasses as he goes from table to table clearing up. Helen and Nancy hold hands and look at each other like they're trying to stop time.

And then the pain in my leg almost makes me jump. I'd forgotten all about it. It sobers me up and suddenly everything looks very clear. I control my body. I keep from making any noise. I breathe slowly.

It's Johnny. Johnny's hand on my thigh.

I look around swiftly. I don't think anybody sees.

I try to make my face blank, even though I want to wince. I lean my mouth to his ear. "Harder."

His fingertips press into my inner thigh and his thumb is almost where the knife went in. The pain sears; my thigh muscle is a slab of meat cooking. The hurt is so hot it's almost numb. The only thought that comes clearly through the burning is the desire not to get a bloodstain on my grandmother's dress. It's probably bleeding again, seeping through the fabric and running down my leg.

As if reading my mind he pulls his hand away, making sure it brushes against my ass on its way to his pocket to pull out a pack of Marlboro reds.

"I'm smoking," he says, trying to sound like he's talking to no one in particular. But I'm the only one in earshot of his flimsy little mumble. Then he turns around to face me, flicks the bottom of the pack, knocking a cigarette out of the top. "Smoke?"

I take it. "Why not?"

I don't really smoke cigarettes. But I can. I follow him outside, not looking at anybody but trying not to look like I'm trying not to look at anybody. Just, you know, *ignoring* them.

Johnny doesn't stop on the steps. He keeps going into the tall grass then, through the grass and over to some boulders overgrown with ivy and moss.

I feel invisible. All I can see around me is the black black night and Johnny, Johnny Come Lately with his salt-and-pepper eye-brows, some of the longest ones I've ever seen, spiking out above his yellow, bloodshot bear-brown eyes. "I love your eyebrows. They're really long."

He looks over his shoulder, just once, quickly, and then plunks his big arms, heavy in his leather jacket, on my shoulders. He moves in fast and plants a longish kiss on my mouth. Then he pulls back to look me in the eye. It feels polite, and there's something very wrong about that. Everything is wrong, so it fits somehow. I take a breath and tilt my head. His cheek nudges mine. The soft skin of his cheekbone contrasts with the scratch of his stubble. I lean in and let my weight fall against him. Johnny's big body is this perfect soft-firm curve, solid and round. It's comfortable and com-forting and I find myself wondering if this is what it's like to have a grandfather. That's not what I mean . . . The most fucked-up thoughts always pop into my head at the worst fucking moments, and this one makes me lose my kissing rhythm and something feels funny against my tongue. And then I realize what it is and I cough a little laugh into Johnny's mouth.

"Do you wear dentures?"

Johnny nods an earnest nod.

"They look really natural." And we go right back into kissing, but only for another minute because a bell rings. Not the chapel bell. I don't recognize it.

"Closing time. Come on."

No, this is all wrong. Something from the Bad Place has made its way into my night and I can't look at him now.

Rose and Gretchen are leaning on the steps. I think they're watching pretty closely when Johnny and I appear from the other side of a big rock and walk back up to the tavern together. Paranoia and liquor bring a bit of scratchy warm puke up my throat.

Rose is holding a joint. "Got a light, big guy?"

Johnny snaps out his Zippo. Rose has a draw and then passes the joint to Johnny. "I think your missus is asking after you. Last call at the bar."

As he goes in, I look through the windows at the stragglers. Everyone's piling up together, smiling, pulling up tables and chairs at the far end of the tavern by the stage. Johnny and Suzie are cuddled up together again. Grover's laughing with Frances and Ernie. Lyall's come out from behind the bar and blows a funny little note into a tuning pipe. The Swans start singing some old English song. Then I get it. This is their closing time song. They all know every word:

Isn't it grand, boys, to be bloody well dead?
Let's not have a sniffle,
Let's have a bloody good cry.
And always remember the longer you live,
The sooner you'll bloody well die.

The Swans start getting their jackets and canes or whatever and make their way out but it can't be time yet. Where's everyone going? It's not that late, surely.

Tiredness is taking over my brain and I wish I could curl up in one of the booths and sleep there. Rose passes me on her way out, gives me a hug and kiss, wishes me happy birthday one last time, and limps off toward her shop.

Black clouds stretch out over the patches of sky where stars still show through. No problem getting back on my own. Except that the stars are spinning faster than usual.

Rumbling noises come at me from the horizon and suddenly I'm trying to get home before it starts raining, and even though I've made this trip eight million times I keep getting lost and finding myself out by the coast instead of on the fast route straight through the middle of the island. The clouds are thickening up over the moon and I can't see anything. My eyes keep closing too. None of this is helpful. The ground under me gets all rolly and crumbly. I've wandered onto the rocks. The sea is black and growling at me, parroting the sky sounds, ganging up on me again.

I left a trail of pebbles but there's no moon to light them up. I left a trail of breadcrumbs but the bad Swans came behind me and ate them all. Can't get back to my grandma's house.

Wait, that's really good. I have to remember to write that down when I get home. They could be song lyrics. Maybe Suzie and Johnny would let me sing with them. Yeah, I should totally be in a band. Sort of mysterious and damaged, a weird young thing in old lady clothes. Life is going to be amazing.

Fuck, it's cold. Where am I? Bugs are biting my ankles. Sometimes waves of heat and nausea take over and I lie down in the grass until my skin feels the cold again and I hoist myself onto my feet and keep going. South, I think, I hope.

We're all going to die. There are moments when I can't see the difference between me and the Swans. We're here together, traveling through time at the same rate, one second per second. Slow as slow gets, but it always feels too fast for me. All of us are moving toward death at precisely the same pace. It's just that they had a head start. They had the sixties and used it all up in just ten years. They used up Morocco and Paris and Venice Beach, Times Square and the Bowery. They used it all, breathed it in deep, down to the end, leaving behind only roaches and ash. Whatever I do will be an anemic imitation of what they did.

But maybe I'm wrong. I've never been to Morocco or Paris. There could be something left, maybe even enough for me. Nothing, then, for anyone who might come next, but I don't think anyone's coming next (although, that's probably what *they* thought). Even if they do, there literally might not be any Paris to go to. Better get it while I can.

By the time I spot Lolly's house I'm shivering and wobbly. The wind has picked up. Down the steps and along the path, trying to keep as far from the edge as I can. I stumble a few times and my heart beats fast as the waves crash hard against the cliff.

The relief is wonderful when I get into the kitchen. I kick off my shoes and curl up on the carpet in the living room. I lie there taking deep breaths until my goose bumps go down and a wave of nausea passes. Eventually I get myself up and I'm making my way to bed when something catches my eye. I double-take. The green light on the answering machine is blinking. It really is. I lunge at it and hit the play button, my heart positively galloping.

The long beep stings. The tape clicks and plays: *Testing, just a test to check that this piece-of-shit twentieth-century technology is still operational* . . . I've never been so disgusted by the sound of my own voice.

I'm so dizzy I can't tell if I'm upright. Somehow I make it to the bathroom, face in the toilet bowl, heaving so hard it feels like I might break a rib until, finally, the first pukey belch breaks through. I throw up three or four times and lie panting on the cool bathroom tiles. Then I'm back at it, stomach squeezing hard against itself, pushing out those last horrible mouthfuls of rancid greenish slime. My face is sweaty and tingling from the strain of it all. I wipe my mouth and teary eyes on a fistful of toilet paper and make my way out on shaky legs.

I go to the guest room, pull the blanket and a pillow off the bed, and curl up on the floor. The blue-gray walls have nothing to do with me. The color is inoffensive and anonymous, like a hotel room. I'm in the middle of nowhere and I could be anywhere. I could be anyone.

The rain starts tapping at the window, gently at first but it gets harder very fast until it sounds more like sheets than drops, a roar that could almost be wildfire. I'm trying to get warm, trying to drift into sleep, but the rain is loud. And after the rain I know what comes next. The ground gets soft and loose, not like the ground should be.

The rain slaps the earth like the silver tail of a sea monster. My house wants to be at the bottom of the sea and it doesn't care if I go down with it. I could be the furniture. I could be a phone that never rings. I'll freeze and bloat. I'll get ripped apart by sharks. And the really frightening thing is how cold it will be, the heat of my blood drifting away as it pours out of me. And the sharks will take no particular pleasure in it. It's like shitting to them. Or like rape. It's only dramatic for the victim. I could be anyone.

Waves slap, dragging their tentacles down the side of my house, spilling their gummy body up and over my roof, belly-flopping hard over me—a giant nightmare jellyfish—before they pull back, bracing for another blow. Smashing, banging, grabbing at me with thick pedo-fingers. It wants me but I'm not ready. And all the air drains back with it. And then the water—the rain, the waves, the flood—comes back. I'll drown before the sharks get me. I once read that drowning isn't so bad. And I'll probably be crushed by the roof or some rocks or something as the house crashes into the ocean. It'll be over soon.

I close my eyes and listen to the waves and the thunder. It's not fair. What am I supposed to do? Walk out in the rain? Hobble over to Rose's place and say, I'm scared of the storm, can I sleep with you? I need this house. I don't have anywhere else to go.

Stop it! You horrible son of a bitch, stop it right NOW! I'm not ready! But nothing I do will make it stop. If it doesn't take my house tonight, the monster's just going to keep coming, growing extra arms until it gets it.

I could make an escape, run for the center of the island and into the chapel while the sea keeps advancing, devouring the island, shrinking Swan from its edges. I'll make for the highest point, climb up the rope, and grab onto the bell. And I'll stay there until the world ends, until the Swans have all gone and the sea has eaten the island all around. I'll stay there forever, sitting on top of the bell, swinging in the breeze when the sun shines, crawling under and hanging from the hammer to keep out of the rain.

My thoughts go black.

CHAPTER TWELVE

Along the horizon it looks like a huge light bulb has crashed and cracked and spilled its light onto the surface of the water. It's . . . it's that something makes you stop and you have to try hard to breathe when you're looking at it. *Arresting*. Waves push forward, lines of white-gloved hands. The sea is gray like a military uniform. White foam advances toward the curve of the coast beneath the cliff.

I sit with my back against the house. The ground is soft and wet from the storm. A damp, gravelly chill is seeping into my underwear and spreading steadily. It's uncomfortable but it feels like I deserve that. I examine the edge of the cliff. Didn't lose too much last night. It's when the air heats up again and the weather dries out, that's when the big slips happen. Not during the storm. In the drama of last night's squall, I'd forgotten. I press my back against the side of my grandma's house and extend my stubbly brown legs out in front of me, stretching my feet, pointing my toes, seeing if I can reach the edge.

Not yet. Soon, though.

I look out across the sea at this day that's just starting. The colors have changed; it's gone all half-assed pastels, nursery colors—powder pink, lemon yellow, peach, lavender, forget-me-not. The sky is baby-talking, trying to trick me into getting excited about doing something that I'm too old to pretend isn't going to be really boring. *This* again—another stupid day in my idiotic life. I can't stand it—I don't want to do this again. Not again. I'm exhausted. I wish it could be bedtime already. It's dawn and I just want this day to end, to have been, and for me to have lived through it. Or I could tumble down, roll over the side and onto the rocks and let the waves finish me off. Surrender is all I have energy for; the prospect makes me feel so much more alive than the thought of making my way from today into tomorrow.

Day, day, go away. Come again another, um. Shit.

After a while, all the interesting stuff stops happening in the sky. There's a dark blue line against the horizon. I'm not sure if I like it. Maybe I do. It creates a kind of cartoonish division between the sea and the sky, keeps you from taking this whole *breathtaking landscape* shit too seriously.

As it gets lighter, the sea is becoming a paler shade but I don't know what you'd call it. Right now the sea is more a texture than a color. Rough: the surface of a painting of nothing. There could be anything under there. Like how poor painters will sometimes paint over an old painting instead of buying a new canvas. Maybe the bottom of the sea is terribly ugly, riddled with errors or just not God's best work. But even I have to admit that that's probably not right. I know there are sparkly things and the sacred geometry of reefs, rubberinesses, spikes, spines, music, etiquette. Just like here, but hidden. Just another place where people like me never go.

I count to three. On three I'll get up. It doesn't work, of course. That kind of thing only works when there's someone else around. She'd clap her hands at me. She thought I was so lazy. *Come on—* clapclapclap—*It's time, now. Get up!*

Marching through the utility room into the kitchen, I decide the only approach is an arbitrary one; just start somewhere. Dishes first. I have to take loads of stuff out of the sink before I can wash anything. I take the rubber gloves from under the sink, turn on the water, and wash them all, dry them all, stack them neatly—*so they nest properly. Don't you dare create those silly balancing acts with my china.* Grease and crumbs like acne on the stove and countertops. I scrub and wipe as many times as it takes. I pull off the knobs and scrape gunk out of the cracks with my fingernails. I put the gloves back on and do the floor, leaning hard on the scrub brush, pushing and pulling until there's no trace of blood from last night. I vacuum the living room, put shit back in its place. I pull out the paring knife I sank in the wall one day when I'd been on the phone for three hours trying to find my folks and the last person I spoke to started laughing when I said their names. Real fucking knee-slapper, son of a bitch.

There's dust in the corners, thick like felt. It's under everything, between all the objects, hanging off the shoulders of ugly figurines. I look at the hard dolls on a shelf, a boy and a girl in the tan burlap of slaves, but with broad white smiles and a healthy, innocent chubbiness to their bodies. Why does anyone make these? Why do people bring these hard, dead things into their homes? Some people find delight, joy in them, or maybe these words are too much—they get a little kick out of them, a tickle, a smile. Do I have anything like that? What do I like?

Upstairs the guest room is covered in dirty clothes and sweaty knots of sheets and pillows. It's all wrong. It's so wrong I can hardly make myself go in. Four of Lolly's watercolors in silver frames hang in a level-straight line like uptight clouds on a *pleasant* day. My computer's on the unmade bed. The blue floral-printed comforter is on the floor, bulky as a boulder next to my dingy socks and once-black T-shirts and crusty underwear, crotch side up. A stack of plates, a mug, some loose change, used tissues, a recordable CD of I can't remember what. My things stand out like an off-black rash against the cool tones of the walls and carpet and furniture. My things don't belong here. And if I start cleaning, clear away the dirty dishes, put the soiled clothes in the washing machine and the clean clothes (ha!) away, I don't know if I'll be able to stand the *pleasant* blue glare of the guest room.

So the next part isn't really cleaning at all, more like picking over the elements of a riddle. Mostly I just pick up the things lying around, overthink them or stare at them like an idiot. I smooth out crumpled pieces of paper, to-do lists, notes to self, phone numbers that ring through to disconnected accounts, ex-friends and fresh enemies of my folks', read them and set them down again. I sniff the armpits of my clothes and look at the stains, picking at them with my fingernail. They're all too big or too small, thermal or wool for a winter that's long gone, failed zippers replaced with lines of safety pins, buttons dangling, hemlines slipping out. I never learned to sew, so my repair jobs make everything I own look like shit.

I try to figure out if my smell is still the same as my parents' smell. I try to remember what they look like. Waiting for a bus in Spanish Harlem, I remember I asked her if she was happy. But I can't see her, can't call her face into my mind's eye. We were the same height by then, and couldn't agree on anything. She just squeezed my arm and exhaled, warm next to my cheek, a hot contrast to the wet bite of the early winter night that blacks out the sky at five in the afternoon, and whispered, "Hush."

The basement studio we lived in then gave us a break from the wind, but not the cold or the damp or the dark. That night I tried to clean up, but grime oozed from the floor and wall, showered down from the ceiling and between the tiles; you could almost see it pushing in to coat us and the furniture, or to crowd us out and move us on to the next place. Pollution settled on the window, almost a kindness because we wouldn't have bought curtains for the single, foot-high slit, a view of passersby stamping the sidewalk.

My mother came out into our single room after a long time in the bathroom. While I cleaned, she stared out that window as if through a veil.

"Look at the snow."

"It's not snowing, Mom. It's raining. It's been raining for a while."

"Which do you like better, rain or snow?"

I had never thought about it before. "Which one do *you* like more?"

"I don't think I've ever seen rain quite like this." Her words moved out of her like the hiss of something deflating slowly. I couldn't be sure if she'd heard my question. "The way it's falling really slowly. It's thick and fat. I think it's snow."

"It's rain, Mom. Just rain."

"It's cold enough to snow."

"That's because we live in a basement, Mother. And just because it's cold enough to snow doesn't mean it's snowing now."

"Yes it does. It's basic physics. Water changes states of matter at a certain temperature. Maybe if you didn't think you were too good for school you'd know about thermodynamics."

"Maybe if my parents cared about my education, I would too."

"Sorry, your highness, if we don't turn into a coach and horses and deliver you to the schoolyard. Or maybe you're looking for us to put you in cuffs and walk you to your classes like death-row screws. You're too old to fuck up and blame it on us."

I was fourteen and didn't argue that last point. I certainly felt old. But not in a good way.

I changed tack, struck back at her. "Where's Dad?"

"Stop."

"It's been a couple of days. Business trip? Or maybe he's caught out in this raging blizzard."

She squared up and looked me in the eyes, her face drawn in grayscale, with blank holes for eyes and nostrils. I could see with certainty that I would die someday. But it wasn't the thought of my corpse, rather my mother's hot palm against my face that shocked me out of my reverie. I heard myself gasp.

She sucked her teeth at me as though I'd just asked her for spare change. I felt skinned by contempt; I needed to cry like a corpse needs to leak but I could only make it if I held my shit together. I took my coat—I couldn't stop to dig for my scarf and gloves among the piles and boxes of what passed for our lives—

and staggered into the dark and falling sky. That smoggy night oozed like cheap chocolate ice cream on dirty blacktop, swirling with pale ribbons of cloud close to the moon. I walked the length of Manhattan, all the way down to Battery Park, breathing in the scent of cold piss and puddles and rough sleepers. I worried about her being home alone, turning on the gas and forgetting what she was doing as the fumes mixed with the sweet stench of cooking smack. But I knew she wouldn't be alone too long. My dad would come back to her and so would I.

I think about that and my mother now. The corpse that was both and neither of us.

I pad through Lolly's room and look in the mirror. My face is wet clay, unformed and gloopy with unctuous smoothness, like eighties saxophone jazz. I wrinkle up with disgust at my reflection. The tension of crying makes my hungover head hurt more, which makes me want to cry harder, and I can't see how life is ever going to get better. Life has tied itself into a heavy knot around my head and bears down hard. Life has me gripped by my fucking face and I can't escape. I can't escape my life; I can't escape my stupid fucking face. The sound of shattering glass hits me before I realize I've balled my hand up tight and punched the mirror.

put my right hand under the running tap in the bathroom and thumb out shards of glass with my left. There's so much blood I'm angry with myself for doing it, but the crunch of the glass against the side of the sink and the way the little slivers scratch as they dislodge from my flesh are satisfying. I grind my teeth along with the sound, squeeze a towel into my hand, bite the plastic off some gauze and wrap up the wound. There's a noise in the distance and then another—two weak blasts from Duck Island—then silence.

I sit on the toilet lid and keep the pressure on my bleeding knuckles. I try to cry but nothing comes out except these *poor me* snivels. The echo of them is like a fly trapped in my head. Trying to cry sitting on a toilet in my underwear and socks was never going to work. I can't take myself seriously. My brain's a piece of fat someone picked off their bacon and tossed back into the greasy pan. My face feels caked in wax.

Codeine. Valium. Water that gets on my face when I stick it under the tap to swallow the pills. I tug a simple gray cotton dress off a hanger in Lolly's closet and pull it over my head awkwardly, trying not to bleed on it. What will I say? How will I make them let me into the meeting, at least? Bat my eyelashes, purr out *please*. Let me in. Please.

I just want to be old like a normal person.

The crack man occupies the full length of the back wall downstairs. A stick figure, really, a negative, a nothing, just the white sky his presence exposes. He's taller than me, but he's not even in my weight class. *You're nothing.*

Just as I start to turn away, a sound makes me look up. It's all wrong, a thunder sound coming from a calm white sky. It's not thunder; it's continuous and it builds until it's so much louder than the other landslips. The growls have shrieks on top, like demons fucking, like worlds grinding against each other.

A second later I know. No, I'm not ready. Stop it now, you horrible fuck! Stop it right fucking now! I bolt to get away, try to get the front door open to escape farther from the slipping cliff at the rear of the house and what's left of the backyard. It hasn't been used for so long that it's stuck. I pull the knob as hard as I can, bracing one foot against the wall and gritting my teeth and trying until my right hand starts to bleed again and I give up and race through the living room and kitchen and out around the back.

I cling to the side of the house, eyes pointed stubbornly upward, and trudge up the hill with the ocean spitting behind my back and the ground shifting, hurling chunks off and out and away. As I trip my way up the broken stairs my hands can't do anything, I can't stop the frames and rewind and edit. My voice is nothing against the roar of hundreds of tons of rock slamming against the rocks below, earth splitting apart from itself, giving in to the waves grabbing at its side, and the cracking and ripping apart of beams and pipes, the whine of the greedy wet mouth of that big blue monster reaching up to swallow my grandmother's house. The dust billows up to scratch my eyes out while I run for a safe distance to watch and listen and wait for the slip to come and pull me in, too.

Heat starts to pull apart the white film stretching across the sky, blue eyes blinking awake. The sea gets excited at the attention. It's behind me but I can hear what it's up to: one hand punching the cliff, others in the swarm clapping at the brutality, froth fingering the little caves and rock pools, breakers draping themselves onto rocks and clinging and pulling like a depressive boyfriend. It pokes into my peripheral vision. I turn my face away but it carries on. It wants me terrified and sputtering, near frozen, eyes and mouth open, laid out for the sea things to check me for freshness before they eat me.

———

The brittle grass digs into the bare skin of my thighs, but it doesn't really hurt when I'm not looking at it or running my fingers over the sore red dents it leaves on the surface. Mostly I'm staring down the coastline in the direction of the house, watching the dust clouds rolling and tumbling like starlings crazed in a swarm. As the dust settles and shifts, the house emerges at the edge of the ragged new coastline. All that noise and it's still standing, but I can't feel as relieved as I know I should. From this distance I can see the rip in the cliff running under the back door. It curves down under the back of the house and then east and around the edge of the island as far as I can see.

The front door is the only way in now. The knob is still stuck. Really fucking stuck. I have to wrap the hem of my dress around it, grip it as blood soaks all the way through the gauze and drips out. Finally the knob clicks and turns and pulls itself out from under my weight, making me fall over the threshold. I'm stiff for a second, paralyzed, wondering if the house can stand the impact of my fall, wondering if I'm still falling.

Inside everything's been rattled off the walls and spilled onto the floor. Picture frames are mostly twin *L*'s on the carpet with hooks and spikes of glass. Lolly's watercolors underneath the debris are just colors and shadows, familiar but they mean nothing. The phone's an upturned turtle by the desk that's given up. The TV's smashed its face in.

I click the light switch but nothing happens. That should have been obvious. I'm not sure whether or not to carry on, whether getting my stuff is actually worth it. It's like I can't work out what surviving means in this context. Finally I decide I'll stick with Plan A until something creaks or shifts under me.

It's hard to lift my legs the height of each stair. There are just as many as there always were, I don't feel like there are more, but the pulling and pressing and lifting of climbing the stairs, the strain of moving without making too much impact against the floor, makes me swear silently at each one, panting, pulse harassing my aching throat. The sweat that runs into the edges of my lips does nothing for my thirst, but the salt is satisfying.

On the last three steps I lie down to push myself the rest of the way, wiping the sweat from my face into the carpet of the landing. And I stay there for a minute, feeling my heart beat into the floor and imagining that I can feel it vibrating through the rest of the house. Wishing for another slip.

Up. I walk into the guest room. One of Lolly's watercolors is still hanging on the blue-gray walls. She was wrong. It really isn't bad. The sky, the texture of the sea, the place where they touch, the air filled with iodine and foam. She used black for almost all of it, letting it dilute in places through all the grades of gray and into nearly nothing. I slip it out of its frame and into my bag. I take my phone and my laptop, and check I've got the envelope with last week's pay. One hundred twenty dollars. Aside from that, there's really nothing here for me. I could take some clothes from Lolly's room, but it's directly over the cliff's edge now and tempting fate to that extent is the same as suicide.

I take out my phone and hit the button to call Jason. He answers after the first ring, which feels like a miracle.

"Hey . . . hey . . ." He doesn't say my name. It sounds like he's moving around. A door closes on his end.

"Jason, it's me." God, he knows that. Obviously, I've called his cell. "Listen, I need to get off Swan for a while and I was thinking maybe I could crash with you?"

"Uh, yeah. When were you thinking? Or maybe it would be better if I just plan to stay on Swan, like, next time I'm out. I could stay over."

"No, it's not that. I need to get out of here and I don't . . . I was just wondering if you could put me up . . ."

He cuts me off. "Okay, but, like, when? Maybe some night next week?"

"I need to leave today."

"Today . . . today's no good . . ."

And he doesn't have to finish. I understand well enough. I've known all along, if I'm honest. I click the red button on my phone. He calls back once. I don't answer and he doesn't call again.

I could have told him. He would have helped if he knew. I know he would, it's not that. It's his tone, the way he said what he said. I knew the real reason without having to ask for it. He has a girl-friend, a real one. They live together on dry, solid land. He loves her, and all this time I've been the one who was imaginary, a girl who doesn't exist on an island no one knows about that's getting smaller all the time.

This is the way the world ends. No, that's not right. What I'm supposed to be telling myself is: this isn't the end of the world. This is not the end of the world. thisisn'ttheendoftheworld. This is *not* the end of the world.

This isn't the end of the world.

I have to go but I'm not ready.

I feel different. I don't know what this feeling is.

My parents are alive somewhere, but I can't wait for them any longer. Maybe we'll bump into each other someday. I hope it's somewhere excellent, the desert, the Louvre, the Taj Mahal at sun-set, instead of the bread aisle in some annoying Podunk supermar-ket, 'cause that's the shitty little town where we've all managed, somehow, to end up.

Will I even recognize them? Would I be able to describe them to the Feds, pick them out of a lineup, identify the bodies? I curl up in bed and close my eyes and don't stop straining until I see them in my mind.

My father is Daniel Edward Freeman. Not too tall, 5'10" or 5'11". Brown hair, brown eyes. Smokes menthols and cracks jokes. He was born on the eighth of August (okay, wait, he was fifty last year, and his birthday hasn't happened yet, so 2015 minus 50 is), 1965. He always liked math and English but he never felt comfortable at school and ended up joining the army. When I asked him about being a hippie in the army, all he said was, "It was a job." I understood.

He spent some time stationed in Germany. I once found a postcard from a woman named Ingrid addressed to Dad but it was in German and I didn't know what it said. He always said he'd teach me to speak German. He taught me a couple of things like *es tut mir leid* and *entschuldigung*. I don't remember what they mean.

He was a boxer when he was younger. He got medals or trophies or whatever for boxing in the army and in prison. I don't know, it seems like he really wants to be gentle, he tries to be, but he just isn't. He's the reason I know how to throw a punch.

He reads all the time, sci-fi books and *Heavy Metal* comics. Those were the only things I can remember being really afraid of as a child. As I got older he started to recommend certain books to me—*Weaveworld*, *Swan Song*, *The Hitchhiker's Guide to the Galaxy*—but I never read them. Maybe I should, maybe they'll help me understand him. I doubt it, though. But I wish I'd read them, I wish I hadn't just ignored him, assumed his books weren't good enough or something. I wish I could tell him I'm sorry. I wish I could have helped him. God, I'm so sorry.

My elementary school friends teased me that my dad was "cute." He has generous, weary smile lines. Tough, tired, friendly, like a cross between James Earl Jones and Che Guevara. I liked him. Yeah, I liked him a lot. No, wait, he was also an annoying pain in the ass. But if we were equals, if he wasn't my dad, I think we'd be friends.

Bella Freeman was born Isabella Sadler on December 30 (okay, Mom's two years older than Dad . . .), 1963. She's a little shorter than me, 5'3" or 5'4". When she was a bit famous it was for her singing, but she's a poet, really, even though she never calls herself one. She even had a book published, a little volume that she said sold well in Haight-Ashbury in the late seventies. She can speak in haikus, which was actually really amazing and hardly ever gets annoying because it's almost impossible to notice unless you count the syllables of everything she says. She can just make up poems, out of nowhere, but she stopped writing them down, which sucks.

She's old-fashioned, even though she doesn't think she is. She'll say things like: I'm a feminist but really now, what kind of woman doesn't cook? But she cooked tough. It was all about knife skills and building the muscles to whisk things to sharp peaks without stopping. We would listen to Patti Smith and the Pretenders and Heart and Fleetwood Mac and twirl and dance each other around the kitchen. Dinner was always late, and when it was really late she'd put down this old pink blanket she had and the three of us would have a midnight picnic on my parents' bedroom floor.

She has amazing breasts. I've even seen photographic evidence that she breastfed me, but her tits—they make me feel optimistic about my future. Maybe it's weird to perv on your own mom's boobs, but it's okay to be sort of hot for your mom if you know how to control yourself. Isn't that what Freud said?

I used to watch her putting on lipstick before she went out. Her lips are thin. She paints them with a little brush. Her nose is narrow, her hair is jet black and silver.

My parents are alive somewhere and I might never see them again. I'm streaming, of course. It's making it hard to breathe. I want to say that I forgive them, even though I don't think that's true. But I do say it, finally. More like a wish.

The day is getting on. I have to go. I have my wallet, though there's nothing much in my account. No driver's license, and who knows where my birth certificate is? Keeping my legs steady as I walk down the stairs is more urgent than thinking about that, though. Downstairs I have another look around but there's nothing it makes sense to take. If I have nothing, no one will believe I'm a real person. Never mind, I have to go.

Outside I stand back a little, plant my feet, and look out to the horizon. The wind laughs in my face. The surprising thing is the beauty of the view, the way the sun cuts through the tears that won't stop coming, the sun like a flamethrower, like an incinerator. The beyond—there's just so much of it I can't believe I'm still breathing. I look down and see the rip in the earth, the gash with some wires and roots and pipes jutting out toward the sea, arms that have lost what they were holding.

More noise rises to meet my ears. If it's another slip, I could just stay put. My first and last big decision as an adult. And then no more. I only have a second, so I think fast.

You know something's a stupid question when the answer pops up just about the same second the question forms. Like: What's the difference between a promise and a lie? Just an age difference, that's all.

And when the question and answer form at the same time, you're just panicking is all, making mental lists of things you already know. It's not the same as thinking.

Like:

They're never coming back—

it's not the same as going down with the ship—

sure people would care, but not many and not much—

oh God, oh God.

Maybe people believe in God because it gives them something to picture. I even go in for it, kind of. Why wouldn't God be some old-ass Santa lookalike, a fat white fuck on his stupid cloud island? It means that if there was a God, he'd have actual balls you could really kick him in and a face to slap and scream in. "You've got a lot of explaining to do! Do you hear me, motherfucker? You've got a lot of fucking explaining to do!"

People believe in God because you can try your best and do everything you're supposed to and nothing happens. God's the sense that real life doesn't make. People believe in God because life is malicious.

"You're doing this to me on purpose!"

Alone in front of the sea and the rocks with my house falling down, I scream my throat to pulp.

Then the noise, the demand, is coming from the other direction. The bell. Someone's ringing the bell. It's time.

At first I'm stumbling, almost crawling, my arms helping me keep moving along the little dirt road as my Tin Man joints ache. Soon I manage to get myself upright, and then to walk and almost run, looking like I've been in an earthquake or a war. Like my house has fallen down.

A glint of blue interrupts my peripheral vision, gagging blue and flecked with froth, and again I turn my face inland, straining, willing the chapel to come into view soon. The sea is the acid belly of a monster who eats dead bodies. We've been feeding it from coastlines and off the sides of boats forever. Walk the plank! Man overboard! Shark attacks, naval battles, plane crashes, tidal waves that take people who were minding their own business (sometimes pretty fucking far from the stupid ocean) and pound suction-cup muscles through the frames of their houses and drag them screaming through coughs of stinging salt water, groping for solid things to hold on to, crying without being able to know they're crying because the salt water the stupid salt water is all over them and it's too similar. Kids who go out too far because they don't know yet what "too far" means and no one told them, not in a way they could understand—just "don't go out too far" without any way to measure how far is "too far," not even a word about how to judge it. It's not like they didn't try, these kids. They did everything right, they weren't trying to be contrary, they just didn't know, and got caught in the undertow. It's not their fault but they're the ones who suffer.

And people love the sea, *love* it, even though everyone knows it's full of shit and garbage and toxic waste and thousands of years' worth of dead bodies. They ride boats across it for *fun*. They get in it, let it touch their skin. They let it up their nose, open their eyes and let it graze their corneas. Well, they can have it. My lungs strain, my legs are a mess of bug bites and nettle stings. I'm sweating in the rising heat, but the sweat dissolves and that's how I like it. Not big-fish-little-fish. Dog eat dog. On land.

The ocean seems like the least attractive place to be a dead body. Water getting into everything, bloating your cells, teasing layers of skin apart. It's a flabby, pallid burial, fish nibbling puny bites, everything inside of you chilled to jelly and oozing out in slow motion. The opposite of a mummification. I'd rather be wrapped up tight, left in the desert to dry. Shrinking in the arid chambers of an actual building, something someone made on purpose. (For all I know, the ocean's an accident, a mistake, a by-product.) In the afterlife the mummies will be the supermodels, skin and flesh air-dried to their skeletons. The sea-buried freaks'll have to develop sparkling personalities to get by.

But I know neither will actually apply to me. I'll die and go into a box, down into the ground where it's dark and quiet but solid and familiar—or into a flaming chamber and then a smaller box and into the air and then (*shit*) probably into the sea. I'll end up as ash-mud on breakers, but I won't be around to care.

When they cremate people, the artificial stuff inside them doesn't burn. I bet they throw away huge boxes of awesome stuff from paupers' cremations. All kinds of pacemakers and silver teeth and plates and pins from broken bones that set badly. When I go back to the Bad Place maybe I'll make sculptures or jewelry from dead paupers' unburned parts, the stuff that stuck around because it was made of different matter.

Two thoughts rush in fast. One is that they probably don't say "pauper" anymore. They probably say "indigent" or something more

PC and less Dickens. The other is a kind of self-scolding: stop thinking about *them*. They're alive. Somewhere. And I'll never see them again. They're not in boxes; they're on a bus or a train or a boat. Their flesh and fillings are in the same place—my mother's skin, smooth and tight over her cheekbones, my dad's forearm muscles and big hands, graying sideburns and gray-brown eyes.

Marie's house appears on the left, good-witch purple with tall stalky wildflowers and grasses and blossoming creepers all but obscuring the paint job. But the usual prog-rock soundtrack doesn't greet me, even when I get really close. The doors are closed in all the little white house-shaped houses with gray roofs, and the Psychedelicatessen is shut up tight with a skull-and-crossbones flag hanging over the porch railings. All the cigarette butts and glasses are gone from in front of the Relic. Rose's grocery looks warm, like she could be inside. I push the door—the bells jingle as I pop my head in—but she's not there. A few more paces up I see her outside the chapel. Swans are filing in. She must hear me getting closer because she looks up, kind of startled. For a second it seems like she might come down and meet me halfway. But she just frowns at me and shakes her head. So I speed up, running to her outside the chapel, frowning too now, trying to remember what I decided I was going to say, but, fuck me, fuck, I never thought of anything, and when I try to open my mouth, just to say, *Please, let me in, please*, Rose very quietly says, "Don't," and goes inside.

Turning away from the chapel means turning toward the ocean. I close my eyes and let my face fill up with salt, over my cheeks and up my nose and down my throat. Drowning.

When I open my eyes, Mrs. Tyburn is holding out a white handkerchief. "Oh, my lamb. My little lamb without a flock. Lost little lamb." The handkerchief is soft and has that clean laundry scent I only normally smell when I'm pilfering Lolly's wardrobe. I want to blow my nose into it but I don't think I'm supposed to. I try to thank her but I just squeak and sob more when I try. She looks like she gets it, anyway.

"I only have a moment, my dear. The others have assembled and we're going to start our discussion."

Do I tell her I can't go back, that it's over? That my house is teetering, slipping, that it could be going over as we speak? "Rose says I can't come."

"And she speaks for us all when she says that." Some things can make your bones twist and break, hammers, daggers, bombs, tidal waves. Mrs. Tyburn sees. "We all know how you feel about the Duchess. And we appreciate that it must be difficult for you to lose someone close to you, yet again. A season in hell, a season in hell."

Her words melt and make me feel more still. The pain that grinds my bones to powder has a name now.

"You must understand, though, that this is not entirely about the Duchess. We're all going her way. *We* are, not you. We're not all going to suffer from dementia, of course, but we are dying of old age, in our own ways, in our time. We've all come out here to die, for ten or twenty or forty or sixty years. Who knows. This place has a purpose, and it is not your purpose.

"If one wanted to wax philosophical, one might say that you're dying too, but not like we are. So, my lamb, as warmly as I and Rose and many of us may feel toward you, this is, to put it simply, not your business. This is no place for you. Now I really must go in. You may keep the handkerchief."

I twist the white cotton and watch her walk away. She's so small it's almost like she's being carried like a piece of pollen in the air.

Sobbing, grimacing, I dig my toe into the dirt. This is how I knew it was going to go. My mind replays it but it doesn't change. I can't even force the image of my having said the right thing, granted a seat at the back or space to stand, being allowed to listen, raising my hand when both sides have had their hearing and the motion is finally raised. I can't see my hand going up to let her go or let her stay and wait.

I head the rest of the way north to the Oceanic. At least, for once, finally, I'll have a chance to really be alone with her. The sea spreads out beyond the lawn, sapphire blue and sparkling incessantly like a Diana Ross drag queen. I head up the wide staircase and across the big porch, which I've never seen empty before, even at night, up the stairs and into the Duchess's room. White flowers, white walls—the breeze through the big window dilutes the pollen's perfume. I sit in my chair next to her, listening to the machines that breathe her lungs and beat her heart. I get my body to beat in time with hers, open my mouth like hers, close my eyes. And because I know it's safe, that all the Swans are eulogizing and yea- or nay-ing down at the chapel, I lift her thin white blanket, and, being careful of her tubes and sacks and things, crawl into bed with her, into the scent of the flowers, and the clack, bleep, suck, drop of her life support, and the breeze, and her soft, warm body. Even she won't stay with me, not even if I beg.

I ask her what to do. I know I have to go, today, right now; my parents might never find me, and I have nowhere else to go. By the time I'm a Wrinkly there won't be a Swan to die on. No Shoals at all. Just ex-ice-cap water and wars in the Bad Place.

New York was awful when I lived there before, and it'll only be more expensive, meaner, with fewer jobs for someone like me—no skills, no diploma. I don't even think I have enough ID to enroll in school if I wanted to. It'll probably smell even worse in summer. And this summer's really fucking hot. Anyway, Manhattan's an island, too. Not a safe bet long-term. Hell, maybe I should move to Detroit or Columbus. The Midwest could be the east coast by the time I'm a Swan. Should I move there and get ahead of the wave? Stake my claim in a safe space on high ground in a little place with a well? Is it too soon to hide out already? There's so much more of the world to see. Will it be scary to be back? Will it have changed too much for me to know how to act? Or maybe it will have been me who changed too much.

Clack, bleep, suck, drop.

What is it like, having the world change so much? From when you were born, I mean. Was it just too much of a leap between the world you first became aware of and the world you were in when your brain stopped firing and popping the way it's supposed to? Maybe it's a kind of exhaustion, so tired you can't think straight, and soon you can't do anything—eat, hold your head up, keep your eyes open. I feel so exhausted I could sleep for a hundred years. But it would be just my luck that I'd wake up and everything would be gone. I'd wake up drowning.

Still, I just want to rest. Without thinking or dreaming. Whatever you're doing, lying in this bed strapped to tubes with tape and needles, it doesn't look restful. If I could have it my way, I would be dead for a week. All I want is a break from existing, something deeper than sleep.

Clack, bleep, suck, drop.

It's time, isn't it? I know. I go to her dresser. Lift the lid on her wooden box of keepsakes. Her driver's license and her Indian Head penny go into my pocket. Her license is still valid. I wouldn't be able to drive with it, but if I needed to use it to apply for something else, like a passport . . . Her birthdate, 1929—I'll say it was a typo, *obviously it should be 1992. Just look at me, come on. You know the DMV; their systems are a mess.* I can picture it—it could work. And the name, Jesus: *Bryony Nuala Euphemia Featherstonhaugh.* No wonder people call her the Duchess. What a fucking mouthful. But lots of people have names they have to grow into. I'll grow fast. The penny is just for luck, *like a brave,* that's what she said. I'm going to need it.

Outside I'm feeling lighter. The day has turned pretty. I spot a cluster of yellow dock and stop on the grass, chew the leaves into a thick green paste, and rub it over the bites and stings on my legs and linger, staring at a bee clinging to a purple thistle nearby. It reminds me of someone sucking my nipples and I laugh out loud, grateful for the joke. It would be nice to have someone to point it out to. Never mind.

There's the ocean. There it always is, waiting for me. And now I have to cross it.

The seagulls bark like guard dogs.

Bells tinkle gently as I let myself into Rose's shop. The earthy smell coats my nostrils. I want to leave her a note or something, but there are no words anymore. Her playing cards are stacked next to the cash box; I fan through and find the queen of spades and leave it on top. I place a nickel on top of that for the three apples I place in my bag. She'll know it's from me, as a thank-you, an *I'll never forget you*. An *I love you*, even. Rose will appreciate that.

I let myself into Mrs. Tyburn's house with her old-fashioned key, tiptoe into the foyer and through to the living room, scanning the ground floor. Fabergé eggs, porcelain figures, the grape shears and olive pitter, a small but really heavy picture frame, a shiny walnut box with satin lining. And the cash she keeps in the drawer by the chair where she has her martini in the evening. Everything is heavy, even the envelope of bills. Everything feels solid and steady, in its proper place. Too easily missed. And I can't be someone who robs old ladies, especially not Swans. I'd be taking much more than fancy eggs and pointless silverware.

I'll have to be quick, the meeting could end any minute now, so I try to focus as I climb the stairs. There's thousands of dollars' worth of equipment in the edit suite, but everything is either too bulky or pointless in resale terms; how much would I even get for used gear that'll be obsolete when the new model comes out next year? Anyway, I have to travel light.

I start up the computer and click through some images for the folder marked *superseded*. Little Sophia is there, cute and round in corduroys that don't fit, trying to smile between those puffy cheeks. She hasn't been to China, not yet. Hasn't developed near-perfect Mandarin or a taste for ducks' tongues and snail porridge.

Just a sweet kid still under her mother's thumb. She looks back at me, not really alive, not really breathing, but nearly; chubby little Sophia Tyburn seems to say there's nothing here for me.

I consider what to do with Mrs. Tyburn's archive. I've only gotten through a fraction of it. Would destroying the rest be the next best thing to finishing the job? Slap-dash but kind, or unspeakably cruel? But I decide that even she can light a match, and the next batch of photos and letters to burn will have to be her own doing. I've done enough so that her past can be whatever she wants, and left the rest in case she thinks remembering is actually worthwhile. I'm still not sure it is.

Past-making isn't my business anymore. I leave Mrs. Tyburn's keys on the table by the door, her past still imperfect in the attic, where it'll probably stay that way. Between Nick's IT "malfunctions" and banking errors, and the Duchess's ID, I have everything I need to mix myself up a new future.

Little rowboats nestle together, red bottoms pointed up to the big blue sky between the tide and the Oceanic. I pull one away from the huddle, turn it upright, and rescue the oars from the ground. I'll row myself out to Appledore and wait for the tourist boat to hitch a ride back to Portsmouth.

This is the break. It's my turn to make a promise, and try my best to keep it. I'll live with not knowing, like other people live with grief. I'll let the part of me that's suffering shut its aching throat and die. I'll let it wash over me. This will be my retirement, the time when I'll learn to want something new, even if nothing ever wants me back.

My face twists like someone with hard, muscular hands is wringing out the tears; they're flowing all over and down into the tense folds. I'm going to have the wrinkles of someone who's been in a lot of pain. By then, none of this will have mattered. When my hair is white and my body's broad and round, the islands will all be different. The maps in my head will look ridiculous.

With the sun showing off behind my back I make a black silhouette on the little waves at the ocean's edge like penguins or babies, innocently disrupting my shape, over and over, never getting tired of the game. In a moment I'll get my feet wet, and that's how they'll stay, in a little boat rowing over to the next doomed little island. I'm as tired as someone ten times my age, but the day's still young.

ACKNOWLEDGMENTS

My heartfelt gratitude to my US and London families for all of your love and support; for the artistic and practical guidance, meals, coffees, crashes on couches, and confidence you offered me, I'm overwhelmed. And Brian Lobel, there are just no words; for everything, forever, thank you.

To Emma Paterson, Sharmaine Lovegrove, Erin Wicks, and Blake Morrison, thank you for the years of guidance and support in bringing this project to fruition.

For their generosity in hosting my research, many thanks to Kane Cunningham and The House in Scarborough, North Yorkshire, and to the Pelicans on Star Island, New Hampshire, whose camaraderie, warmth, and feistiness I deeply admire.

Thank you to Dan Paz, Chipp Jansen, Martin Chapman, and Christopher Halliwell for sharing your expertise in analog and digital technologies, software, hardware, malware, and all things blockchain.

Finally, I am so grateful to Arts Council England for their generous support of this project.

ABOUT THE AUTHOR

Season Butler is a writer and artist born in Washington, DC. Season also works as a dramaturg, and as a lecturer in performance studies and creative writing. She lives and works between London and Berlin. *Cygnet* is her first novel.